Another Day

KRISHNAN IYER

RG
books

Published By

Redgrab Books Pvt. Ltd.

942, Mutthiganj, Prayagraj, 211003

www.redgrabbooks.com

contact@redgrabbooks.com

Price in india : 225/- INR

First published by Redgrab Books in 2024

Copyright © 2024 Redgrab Books Pvt. Ltd.

Copyright Text © 2024 Krishnan Iyer

Printed and bound in India

Cover Design & Typesetting by Redgrab Books team

ISBN : 978-93-95697-53-8

Let us talk

You see, in all the instances, unlike our usual thinking that trouble finds us, something that I too do because it is easier to feel like a victim of circumstances, or of the villainy of others, the fact is that I keep looking out for trouble, and I easily find it. That trouble likes me, is a realization that I have had only now: when I am already forty-seven. It visits me every other day. Like the other day, I had tooth ache, and I had to visit my Dentist. Earlier, I would be very frustrated by trouble's visits but only now, that is, when I am a full seventeen years inside the zone between 'not young anymore' and 'not yet old' (do you remember the old TV commercial selling us vitality pills called 30 Plus? This means that after thirty, we need pills. Otherwise, why wasn't that pill called 35 Plus, or 40 Plus, or 45 Plus?), I am coming to realize that each visit of trouble is to give me some deep enlightenment like the tooth pain eventually gave me the realization that Dental work is really expensive and that I should have visited the Dentist for regular checkups when I did not have any pain.

Even though I don't seek out troubles yet I have had many troubles, and they have all added to my wisdom. This is not to say that I have started to enjoy my troubles in the way that athletes enjoy their muscle aches. This is to say that I could do nothing about them and therefore, I tried to learn from them so as not to get into more troubles. But like amoeba, trouble takes a different shape each time and it dodges my filters.

Now, like in a lesson where some pupil may get it and same won't, troubles may enlighten some, and some will just keep scratching their heads. But then, you need losers also if you need to come out as the winner. When you are a winner, you have the trouble of dealing with the losers – their whining, their crying, their calling you a cheater, and all. There is trouble in winning too. Trouble is everywhere. This is why, wise old people and young motivational speakers talk about facing the troubles because they know that troubles cannot be avoided.

Trouble is such a great thing that if you don't have any trouble, it will make you realize that that too is a trouble that you don't have any trouble. See, The Buddha was a prince and his father made sure that he had no trouble. Then one day, he realized his trouble that he did not have any trouble, and so he set out to have all kinds of troubles before he was totally enlightened. But then, what of his enlightenment? The troubles that enlightened The Buddha still remain. People still become old, sad, infirm, and die. So, I have come to realize that the only truth out there is trouble, which is to say that truth is trouble and trouble is truth, and that every day is another day.

My name is Durga Prasad Jha. Can there be any trouble in that?

Most of my friends, including those from work, call me DP which sounds quite suave. A good name can do that to people that is, add some style to them. But name can act otherwise also. When I joined my MBA class, there joined with me another Jha – Abhijit Kumar Jha. His name would come before mine in any list that was put in alphabetical order. He became Jha-One, and I became Jha-Two, as people would shout out to call me. This may not be a trouble for everyone but it became one for me because any proper noun, when called out in English, may actually be a word in some language. Only Srinivasan did not understand my problem because he did not know Hindi. But, that was only until someone explained Jha-Two to him. "Hey maccha *Jhatoo", is how Srinivasan starts any conversation with me even today because one day, which was otherwise just like another day, Abhijit Kumar Jha joined MBA in my batch, in the same section.

*Jhatoo is a cuss word in colloquial Hindi.

PART 1

Love and City, can be left in a jiffy

You know that trouble and I find each other. That is why, in our weekly conference calls, when I know that my boss likes brief updates, I still go into a roundabout verbose babbling, and then I get it from him to the sniggers of others. Likewise, when the pursuit is of only money, when I know that no one has as yet become rich by changing jobs, and that all jobs are more or less equally frustrating, demeaning, killing, sucking, I change jobs. In the few times that I have done this, one was many years ago when I decided to not only change my job but in changing it, decided to relocate from Bangalore (that is how it was known until it became Bengaluru) to Mumbai, which was a decision of which, when people became aware, some exclaimed with horrific incredulity, some kept silent, and some said " best of luck" because unlike some decision one takes about which others immediately give their sanction like "he is one lucky chap" when one betroths a possessor of beauty, in certain matters, people reserve the showing of their judgement for a prospective time to eventually either say "I told you so, this won't work out" or say " I knew it was the right decision", depending on the outcome so that they are always right in retrospect. The missus was happy because her folks lived in Pune, her folks were happy because their daughter was coming close to Pune: to Mumbai.

Before we moved to Mumbai, I had already leased a two-bedroom apartment at Chheda Nagar in Chembur. I chose this place because it was nice, of course, but more importantly, it was affordable for me, and that gave me the impetus to rationalize further on why it was the best place by finding it to be conveniently located to travel around the city of Mumbai by being almost in the center of it.

At first, I came to Mumbai all alone leaving the missus and our two small children, the girl all of two and a half years and the boy, an infant of six months in Bangalore. Like every employer who relocates an employee, my employer too gave me free accommodation in Mumbai for 10 days within which, I was to make my own arrangement for stay. Since I wasn't a high-ranking employee, I wasn't put up in a swanky hotel or anything at Nariman Point or Bandra. I was accommodated at a serviced apartment in Versova.

Versova is in the western suburbs of Mumbai which has a high quotient of glamour. The close neighborhood includes Juhu with its famous beach, five-star hotels where the movie stars and the star kids frequent, and Amitabh Bacchan's twin bungalows. Abutting it is Andheri West with its large apartment communities that house the rich, the corporate honchos, the television stars, wannabe actors, models, where there are film production houses and studios, upmarket gymnasiums where the body is maintained not as the house of the soul but as the implement of livelihood with its six pack and lean look. In such an environ, even the modest prefer to wear their trousers a bit tight, the hem not going below the ankles, the hair coiffured in the latest style, the voyeuristic eyes hidden behind dark googles, and a sling bag running across the torso to hang a bit low at the hip. The dazzle of Versova was too much for my middle-class sensibilities because people like me, who are modest by means and not by virtue, are usually prigs who carry disdain for the not so well off by seeing them as uncivilized, and carry contempt for the really well off by seeing them as vain and uncultured. I knew that I couldn't afford

Every Day is Another Day

living in Versova.

On the third day of my allocated 10 days, which was a Wednesday, I called Subbu whose mobile number was already in my phone's contact list. It was already high time that I called him. The day I told the missus that I had got the new job, and that we would have to move to Mumbai, she had immediately called her mom, and before I had even taken off my shoes and walked inside to our room, she had turned, extended her hand to give her phone to me and said "Papa wants to talk to you", who, the moment he heard me from the other side said "You talk to Subbu. He is a very good property agent. You tell him my name. He will show you some good places. I will SMS his number to you".

"Hello, Mr.Subbu", is how I started our conversation when he picked up his phone. "Yes Saar, yes Saar", he replied. I told him about my father-in-law and he instantly recognized him. "Aiyyo! Saar is a very old friend Saar. You are his son-in-law, very good, very good. Saar had called me Saar, and he said you will need a two-bedroom apartment. I have in mind some good ones Saar in very good areas", he said.

Me: In which areas can you help me find a good house?

Subbu: In Chembur, Saar.

Still a greenhorn about the city of Mumbai, I did not understand how far he was asking me to come from Versova. Before I could ask anything further, Subbu asked if I could come the next day?

Me: Tomorrow is not possible. I have to go to office. How about the weekend?

Subbu: Wokay, wokay, Saar. Saturday you come around eleven in the morning. Where are you put up Saar?

Me: Versova.

Subbu: Aiyyo! Versova!

Me: Why? What happened?

Subbu: Nothing Saar. On Saturday, you will come by train na Saar?

Me: No, I will take a taxi.

Subbu: Wokay Saar, you leave by 9 O' clock Saar. Then only you can be on time.

Aiyyo!, this time I exclaimed.

On Saturday, I hired a taxi from a taxi stand close to the serviced apartment in which I was put. I hired it for the whole day so that we, that is Subbu and I, could use it conveniently to move around and see all the apartments that Subbu said he would show me. "Bala, Saar", is how be introduced himself when I met him near Amar Mahal at around 11 AM. "But I have been calling you Subbu", I said. "Saar, my full name is Balasubramanium. It is long no Saar, so some people call me Bala, some call me Subbu, my relatives call me 'Kondai', that is my pet name. Many names Saar", he said and laughed at the same time, ejecting a spray of spittle. I swallowed my disgust, and took out my kerchief to wipe my face.

Bala did not provoke much confidence in me but his overall docile appearance betrayed his desperation, and I understood that he won't be able to make unreasonable demands in the way property brokers do. From where we were standing next to our taxi, I could see

10   *Every Day is Another Day*

the big sign board of Shopper's Stop. "Come Saar, we will first go to Tilak Nagar, I will then show you two flats very close from here at Pestom Sagar, and then, we will go to Chheda Nagar", he said before we sat in the taxi and started our house hunting.

Bala did take me to see all the apartments that he had mentioned in Tilak Nagar and Pestom Sagar. They were all nice but none seemed to beckon me the way the last one did when we came to Chheda Nagar. Like a promontory, Chheda nagar juts out of the mainland where the Mankhurd Ghatkopar link road and the Eastern Express highway meet. In this way, it is right in the middle of the city but still maintains a silent and secluded existence. The house belonged to Mrs.Swaminithan who was staying in Chheda Nagar for old time's sake despite the urgings of her sons, who now lived in Goregaon, to come and live with them. But now, Mrs.Swaminathan couldn't say no anymore to her sons because age was catching up with her and pragmatism was winning over sentimentality. She was an amiable looking lady in who, I saw the first sign of approval when she saw me take off my shoes before entering her house. When Bala asked for some water, she got it in two short and stout steel tumblers found in South Indian homes. I took mine, and instead of putting it to my lips, I lifted the tumbler above my head, bent my neck, and poured the water in my gaping mouth. When I brought down the tumbler, Mrs.Swaminathan was standing still in front of me holding the salver in which she had brought the water with that look which only old people can give when, despite their loss of faith in the generation that came after them, they get some hope, on seeing an act of which they approve, that all is not yet lost. She did not bother herself much and let Bala show me around the house. It was on the ground floor of the first building inside a community that had two rows of four buildings, each building having four floors. It was a two-bedroom apartment that was larger and more spacious than any of the other apartments I had seen earlier that day. Owing to the large shutters that ran the entire length of the living room, the house had good amount of natural light which I liked. When we returned to the living room, Mrs.Swaminathan was sitting on the cane sofa, which, I was to learn shortly, she would be leaving behind, along with the beds in the bedrooms, her old Samsung refrigerator and washing machine, an old CRT television, again from Samsung by way of letting out what people smartly call a fully furnished house when they leave behind their old stuff not so much for the benefit of their tenants but for their own convenience of not having to lug around their old and out of fashion belongings, like in the way the sugar mills first extract all the juice from the cane to make themselves money and then some more by selling the bagasse. "Your house is very nice Maami", I said having picked up the salutation from Bala who would call Mrs. Swaminathan 'Maami' whenever he spoke to her. She said "thank you" before she went on to let me know how Mr. Swaminathan had come to Mumbai in 1968 to do odd jobs in the city before finding permanent employment, after which, she too came from their village in Palakkad, with their son and daughter to join him here, the family got extended further when her younger son was born in 1972, that they all lived in a one room tenement in Sion before Mr. Swaminathan bought this apartment in 1985 after many years of saving money, Sundari, that is her daughter, now lives in the US with her doctor husband, Mani, her elder son works at a shipping company in Colaba, Venkat, her younger son, who is also her youngest child, works as a senior executive in a foreign bank having its office at Nariman point, and that both her sons live in adjacent apartments at Goregaon East near the Film City to where, she would be going immediately after she finds a good family to lease out her house. In knowing all of this, what I actually took away that day was that perhaps there comes a day in everybody's life when more than anything else, the one thing that one needs the most is someone to talk to. In addition to this learning, I did not know that by listening to her without once interrupting her, I had already made that penultimate mark on her to get her approval before one last thing which she enquired with quite some tact when she asked "what kind of food do you like?", and I, the smart cookie that I am, picked up the cue and said "only vegetarian" to which, sighed not only Maami but also Bala. "Maami, I need to bring my family here in a week's time. If you agree to give the house to me, can I do that? It will be the 23rd of this month", I said. "Yes, as soon as we finalize, I will just take my clothes, empty the kitchen, and go to Goregaon", she said. "Maami, how much is the rent?", I asked. "All that I don't know. Venkat has told Bala everything. He will tell you", she said looking at Bala after having spoken to me. "Wokay Sir, we will speak outside in the car", he said.

On the 23rd of September in the year 2007, which was a Sunday, by the afternoon flight that landed at the domestic terminal of The Chhatrapati Shivaji Maharaj International Airport in Mumbai at 2 PM, the missus, our little girl, our boy who was still a baby in arms, and I arrived with three large bags that had our clothes, toiletries, and footwear for immediate use. Ram Avtaar was waiting for us at the airport in his Taxi which was an old and battered Premier Padmini. Ram Avtaar is the same taxi driver who had brought me from Versova to Chembur earlier on the Saturday I came there to look for a suitable house. As it happens in Mumbai where everyone seems to have a keen sense of business, on that day, during our return trip, Ram Avtaar had asked me to save his phone number and call him anytime I needed his service.

I had reached Bangalore on Friday morning. It wasn't counted as a leave for me but I was let to take care of my shifting. As such, I wasn't moving any mountains within these early days of my new employment. That I had got a 'fully furnished' house in Mumbai had created a new challenge for me which was of taking care of my own household stuff that collectively were my TV, refrigerator, washing machine, sofa set, cots and all. But then, the way one often times finds Iodex already at home when one twists the ankle in the way that the remedy was waiting in anticipation of the problem it was to solve, I too found the solution: which was close at hand.

Late in the year 2004, when the missus was already carrying our first child within her, the pressure on me was mounting to buy our own house because now, we were on the family way and not having a house of our own would never qualify us as having settled in life because it was the last item to be ticked in the long list of expected items of a seemingly happy and successful life – education, job, marriage, child, house. When we started to look for suitable houses to choose one from, we found the houses that we liked to be way beyond what we could afford because houses then were apartments in swanky communities with a swimming pool, a gymnasium, walkways, lawns and all (which the software engineers had made the common denominator after their international exposures to the USA and to Europe and which, they could afford with their dollar earnings and employee stock options) after seeing which, the missus and I did not like the simple ones that were affordable in Bangalore. While I could remain stoic in this frustration of not being able to afford what I liked which, in a way, was a hard punch to my self-esteem, the missus would call her parents in Pune after every unsuccessful visit to new construction sites. Not being able to withstand any further the distress of their daughter, my father-in-law suggested that we buy a house in Pune instead of in Bangalore. Therefore, spurred by the wisdom of my father-in-law and the fastidiousness of my missus, we went to Pune for a quick visit where, my father-in-law took us to a few construction sites he had already identified from which, we booked our house - a three bedroom swimming pool facing apartment on the third floor of the fifth building of nine seven storied buildings in an upcoming community called Green Towers at Wakad, which wasn't too far from my in-laws' house, and right off the Mumbai-Bangalore highway. The house cost me less than half of what I would have had to pay in Bangalore. Of course, I took a home loan from HDFC Bank. I got possession of the house in June of 2007 and in July, four bachelors working in Infosys jointly leased the apartment which was just walls and floor without any furniture and fixtures other than the plumbing, the lights and the ceiling fans. So, we decided to move all our stuff, other than the things of the kitchen and our clothes, to Pune and make the stay of the bachelor boys a bit comfortable where, they took the monkey on their back and also agreed to raise the rent a bit for the TV, the washing machine, the refrigerator, the sofa, and the cots they were to get.

As arranged, the folks from the 'movers & packers' came around ten in the morning on Saturday. By 3 PM, they had emptied the entire house and loaded all our stuff in the truck. It was arranged that the truck will go to Pune and all the furniture will be taken to our apartment there and arranged. The kitchen stuff, the crockery, the bedsheets, the pillows, the blankets, the quilts, the missus' so many saris and dresses, shoes and chappals (that were bought with great enthusiasm but which did not serve any useful purpose and which, we were neither able to throw away nor give away because they were bought with honest, hard earned money and so, we would carry them around in the way a stray dog can sometimes be seen playing with some piece of trash until the thing of its interest is ripped and frayed by its vigorous play) and my books were all packed in about fifteen cartons marked for Mumbai. All the household stuff was supposed to reach Pune on Wednesday. The cartons, we were to receive in Mumbai on either the next Saturday or, a day later on Sunday.

By 2:30 PM, we were already in Ram Avataar's taxi. In about forty-five minutes, we reached our new home where Bala, after I spoke to him on his phone on landing in Mumbai, was waiting outside the community's gate, talking to the old security guard there, with the keys.

After seeing us inside our new house, Bala gave me the phone number of a nearby hotel to order our food. I ordered a couple of masala dosas for us and the simple daal khichdi for our daughter because it was already late in the afternoon, and if things had to be ordered from outside, I wanted a more elaborate meal for dinner. Bala took our leave after saying "any help Saar, just call me." By this time, it was already close to 4 PM. I sat down on the cane sofa under the ceiling fan. It wasn't so hot then. The monsoon had almost receded but there still was a lot of humidity in the air. It was feeling nice under the fan. The missus was somewhere inside. Just then, I heard the cry of my boy who was sleeping in the bed in the master bedroom. "See, if you can get milk somewhere close by", the missus shouted from the inside. I got up from the sofa. Just then, she came out holding our boy: our girl walking behind her. "Take her also with you", she said referring to our girl, who was much excited about the prospect of going out. I took hold of my daughter and walked out in search of milk. Strolling at a leisurely pace, walking along the directions given by the security guard, I found the shop, bought milk, and returned home tracing back the path I had taken to come to the shop.

When I entered our building, the missus was outside the door in the common passage, speaking with a lady who was similarly outside her door which was of the apartment next to ours. The missus was holding the feeding bottle that was filled with milk. As soon as she saw me, she said, "O! he is here". It was a no brainer for me to get that this was our neighbour. Since my hands were full, I could not join them but I immediately said "Namaste". Our new neighbour smiled broadly. "This is Lakshmi Maami. So nice she is. When she heard the baby cry, she knocked, and though I kept saying no, she just did not listen and took the bottle to get some warm milk. We are so lucky to find such nice people", the missus said. Just then, a very plump boy, who did not appear to be more than ten years old, came from somewhere inside his house and stood behind Lakshmi Maami holding the end of her Sari. "Ganesh, say hello to uncle and aunty", she said. Ganesh did not say anything but kept on staring ahead at me and my daughter, who was still holding my hand. Lakshmi Maami also did not prod him further while we all stood there for a few seconds, without saying anything. Just then, the delivery boy from the hotel came with our food. He looked at all of us tentatively extending the white polythene bag in his hand through which were visibly bulging the puffed packets of sambaar and coconut chutney, and asked "101?". I immediately answered "haan, haan, idhar". The missus pulled our daughter towards us. I pulled out my wallet from my back pocket, paid for the food in cash by pulling out two hundred rupees bills because the bill amount was one hundred and eighty, in my magnanimity said "change rakh lo", took the food packet from him and looked up when, Lakshmi Mami said "okay, you have your food", smiled again, turned, pushed Ganesh back inside her house, followed him, and shut her door.

I followed the missus and our daughter inside our new house. Swaminathan Maami was very considerate, and other than her most essential things like the mixer grinder, the wet grinder, and some large woks and vessels that left patches on the lowest shelf in the kitchen in their wake when they went with her, she left behind most of her utensils as well so that we had the bowls to empty the sambaar and the chutney, and the plates to have our masala dosas. By the time we were finishing our meal, it was nearing five, late in the afternoon, the time that is the harbinger of evening, when, from the window in the living room where we had pushed the sliding shutter considerably, a slight breeze wafted inside, soothing us while we were squatting on the floor, eating. As the evening dawned, the missus, who by then, rummaging through the stuff Swaminathan Mami had left behind, found a small brass diya. She sent me out to get a packet of cotton wicks, a small bottle of oil for the diya, a little sugar, and matchboxes. I got all the things she asked, including the fragrant oil purported for lighting lamps, from the same shop from where, a little earlier, I had bought the milk. As the twilight descended, in front of the small statue of Ganesha that was kept in a slot in the wall unit in the living room, the missus lighted the lamp after which, she went to the kitchen while I sat in the sofa, took my daughter in my lap, and switched on the TV to check if the cable subscription was still working, which was in fact working because as soon as the set top box was switched on after the TV, some incomprehensible sounds came and on the screen, a moustachioed man in checks shirt was reading news, perhaps in Tamil, because on the top right of the screen, the logo of SUN TV was visible which, most likely, was the channel that Swainathan Mami was watching before she last switched off the TV. I kept on pressing next until suddenly, NDTV came where again, it was some news only but in English which I could understand. The missus called from inside the kitchen. I put my daughter next to me on the sofa and got up. When I went to the kitchen, the missus had boiled some milk in a small vessel such that it had risen up and spilled a bit on the gas stove after rising above the brim which it will always do unless one turns off the knob at the nick of time but this time, it was let to spill over in the ceremonial way of boiling milk when one enters a new house, even though a rented one. Such customs are still alive, courtesy the cellular phone by the grace of which, the likes of my missus can speak to their mothers who pass on the traditions to their daughters via satellite. The missus poured some milk in a steel cup and took it to the living room to keep it next to Ganesha as oblation before she came back to the kitchen, poured some milk in a steel tumbler and gave it to me to drink, which I did, and so did the missus, after which, we came back to the living room, while our boy slept peacefully in the master bedroom, picked up our daughter from the sofa, stood by the open sliding shutter seeing outside, where the lights were already on, the paved rectangular space enclosed by the buildings looking busy with the parked cars, some people walking around this quadrangle, a child pedalling its tricycle while its mother was walking behind, a thin looking man standing next to his bicycle on the back carrier of which was tied a bamboo basket that had jasmine strings that he was selling, that South Indian women like to wear by braiding them in their hair or, by putting them around their bun, all sights that, in their coming together, adumbrated the prospective happy times.

"See, we were living in Bangalore until yesterday, and today, we are standing here in a different city. How fast things happen", the missus said casually but which sounded grave. I looked at her and smiled.

Just two days, which, even though it appears less, is a very sufficient time to shift the household and move to a new city because all one has to do is to quickly pack all the stuff, load it in a truck, and leave. That is all it takes to severe one's ties with a city like it is the case with any separation where all the time spent in seeking the notice of the muse, to get past one's own tentativeness and dithering, express one's love, and the long courtship when that love is requited, do not get a single moment of thought when one says, over some trifle, "it's over, we are breaking up". Our break-up with Bangalore had happened, and without much thought to how that city had opened its arms to us when we first moved there, we moved on.

The in-laws come

Things settled quite fast for us. For the missus, on our very first morning in the new house, Lakshmi Maami sent her domestic help to take care of the jhadu-pocha and bartan, which are the most despised chores in Indian households. The missus was very happy. It was now not possible to call Ram Avatar who was very far in Versova. However, this was Mumbai, and on Monday, when I was returning from Lower Parel after meeting a prospective client, on reaching home, the taxi guy asked me if I would be needing to commute regularly, and when I said "yes", he gave me his phone number because he was from Govandi, which is very close to Chheda Nagar. This was a Sardar named Lucky Singh. This way, very soon, the matters of the household and of conveyance, the former being the most critical problem to be assuaged for conjugal bliss, and the latter being just behind finding an affordable house in Mumbai, got fixed.

While we were expecting our cartons to come by Saturday, we were pleasantly surprised to receive them on Wednesday itself. On Friday, I reached home around 7:30 PM. As soon as the missus opened the door, and I stepped inside, she said "mummy and papa are coming tomorrow morning to help with the unpacking. "While this was good, the only issue it created was that like most people on the other side of sixty, my in-laws would get up early and get fidgety, which meant that they would leave from Baner in Pune by 6 AM in their car to reach early, which further meant that I had to get up not later than 7 AM, unlike what one plans for a Saturday.

I got up not because of the alarm but because I started to perspire, and before I even opened my eyes, I realized that someone had switched off the ceiling fan. Since the switch was located high, it would have been a deliberate and sadistic action by the missus only, I knew. I opened my eyes and looked up at the wall clock. It was 7 AM. As I was still lingering in bed, the missus walked in and said 'Utho, time ho gaya. Mummy, papa have already left at six.", before she walked back to the kitchen from where, I could now hear the sounds of dishes and vessels being washed, which was earlier than usual.

I was still in my bed when the missus returned with a cup of coffee. I sat up. In the next hour, I was ready having finished my bath as well after helping my daughter brush her teeth. As I was putting on my t-shirt, my baby boy cried out, the missus shouted from the inside "see to him", and no sooner I picked him up and came to the living room than, the doorbell rang, and with the baby still in my arms, when I opened the door, there, standing in front of me was my mother-in-law who, even before she noticed me, snatched my boy from me, showered him with kisses on his cheeks, started to speak to him in some strange language that had a lot of alle le, oho oho, aaja aaja, mera beta, mera bhaiyaa, mera raja, when suddenly, from behind her, came in an unmodulated voice ' andar to chalo pehle', to which I moved a bit away, my mother-in-law walked in, and there, standing with a small suitcase in one hand and a canvas bag in the other, wearing a white half sleeve shirt, brown trousers, and leather chappals, was standing, my father-in-law, who walked in, looked at me and said " go and see if I have parked the car correctly?", before he sat down on the sofa and muttered "very hot" while wiping his face with his palm. When I came back, I entered home to a cacophony of excited voices. My in-laws, the missus, the children, were all together in the living room, all trying to speak to one another, even the baby boy was babbling in between. My in-laws had taken the sofa, my daughter was sitting in my father-in-law's lap, my boy was in my mother-in-law's arms, the missus had taken one arm chair. I

Every Day is Another Day

sat in the other and asked my father-in-law "how was the drive?" before I said "you found the house without any difficulty". "Until I stopped work, I used to come to Mumbai very often. This drive is very familiar to me. And, Chembur and Chheda Nagar, I know very well", he said. "You had breakfast?", I asked. "Mummy has brought Poha and Sattu ka Paratha", the missus answered. "Come mummy, we will take out the breakfast", the missus said, got up, picked up the canvas bag that was near the sofa, and went to the kitchen with my mother-in-law following her with my baby boy still in her arms. This left me alone with my father-in-law, who is a very nice man but for the many questions he keeps asking me as though interrogation is the only way of communication, he prefers with me. While this line of conversation was going on, the missus said, from inside the kitchen, "open the dining table na" to which, I got up and opened the wall mounted folding table that was on the right of the TV unit, and pushed the two Neel Kamal plastic chairs close to it. Soon thereafter, the missus came with a bowl that had Poha in it, and a steel plate that had a thick stack of Sattu Parathas, things that the mother-in-law had brought from home, she arranged these on the dining table and returned to the kitchen to come back again with some butter and a bowl of Dahi. We all ate very well.

The thing about any meal, where it is supposed to energize us because it is the fuel for the body, opposed to what it is supposed to do, in most people, is that it induces slothfulness, perhaps because in the most basic sense, all our industriousness is directed towards earning our food, and when that has been found, the body wants to relax, and the mind wants to switch off. Induced by such a post meal inertia, I came back to the living room, sat in the arm chair, reclined against the cushion after sliding a bit, and extended my legs forward. My father-in-law had finished his breakfast, and he did not come back to the living room. I switched on the TV. The missus came to the living room and said, "keep the volume low. Papa is sleeping". "So much for helping with the unpacking", I thought. Anyway, most of the unpacking was already done. My books had already gone inside the overhead loft in the smaller bedroom, the missus just couldn't wait to take out her dresses and saris, and the footwears were all stacked in the shoe rack outside the house, which was also the courtesy of Swaminathan Mami.

The missus was all for ordering lunch from outside however, like every mother, my mother-in-law found her child's ways as profligate, and said "no, no, for just the few of us, what is the difficulty in making some daal, subzee, and roti. You go and sit. I will make them". I was still watching TV when the missus came to the living room with a steel plate having some savouries and sweet. She gave the plate to me and said "ye na, papa has brought. This is Lakshminarayan ka chivda, Chitle ka Bhakarvadi, and Chitle ka Shreekhand. I took the plate and started munching. The missus sat next to me and said " listen, get some vegetables please", to which, when I said "order lunch from outside", she narrated her conversation with her mother, and so, on an otherwise blissful Saturday morning when I was just eating and lounging, I had to get up, take a canvas bag, put on my chappals, and go out to buy some vegetables with my daughter in toe because as soon as she sensed that I was going out, she came somewhere from the inside and clung to me.

I returned home in about 20 minutes having bought a large cauliflower, a kilogram of potatoes, some tomatoes, a couple of cucumbers, a quarter kilogram of carrots, and the mandatory Dhaniya and Adrak, and since Chheda Nagar is a predominantly South Indian locality, the guy at the vegetable shop, who was in a blue checks lungi that was tied at his waist but folded up to his knees, holding there all the while, which is a fantastic feat sans any kind of fastening in a lungi like buttons or straps, put in some curry leaves also, for free. Before I left the shop, I had a tender coconut as well, not so much because I had any thirst but because, someone was having one, and often times, an urge swells up to drink or eat something just by seeing someone drink or eat that thing, and adding to that, I got fascinated by the dexterity of the lungi man who, while I was entering his shop, was holding a large coconut in his left hand, slashing it with a sharp hacking knife held in his right hand, rotating the coconut after each hack, such that by the time it completed one full rotation, it's top was shaved clean, a conical head appeared, at the tip of which, the lungi man, with the tip of his knife, chipped away a small bit to get a small round opening in which, he put a plastic straw, and handed over the coconut to the expectant customer to sip from it, before asking me "Sir, what do you want?"

After keeping the canvas bag in the kitchen, as I was coming back to the living room, from the passage, I peeped inside the smaller bedroom. My father-in-law was just stirring in the bed, after his short nap. The missus and her mother were in the bedroom. Despite their daily long phone calls, they still had a lot to talk. I was once again watching TV. From the corner of my eye, I saw my father-in-law come out of the bedroom and walk towards the kitchen, perhaps to have some water, because I heard the sound of water pouring in a tumbler from the Aquaguard. When he came to the living room, he was carrying the chopping board and a knife, while my mother-in-law walked behind him carrying the cauliflower in her hand and a few potatoes in a steel bowl. May father-in-law sat down on the floor in the middle of the living room, and my mother-in-law kept the vegetables near him. "Give me a peeler", he said to her as she was turning to go back. This was a man who had retired from The State

Bank Of India as a General Manager, who used to sit in large cabins during his different positings, who would lord over his subordinates, who got driven around in an official vehicle, who got to live in some of the finest government accommodations, and now, after he retired, while he still carried the airs about him, was tasked with chopping vegetables, without any hesitation, because, when people wistfully think about their retirement as those days when they will live peacefully, forget that even after their retirement, for them, the days will continue to have twenty four hours, that after late in the morning, they may not have much to do, their ample rest will come in the way of another round of sleep because they won't be able to sleep again, and therefore, in the absence of carefully cultivated interests or fraternities to keep themselves engaged, will have to stay home most of the times, and help with the chores. The General Manager had become a Gharelu Man. While there is nothing wrong with that, and helping in the chores is a virtue every man should have, the GM becoming a different kind of GM was a nice thought I got that amused me.

In the evening, my father-in-law took us all out to khau-gali in Ghatkopar (East) for his old time's sake. On Monday morning, the in-laws left for Pune at 7 O'clock.

The Sandwich Massage is available in Mumbai

The week that started was not a very hectic one because it was the first week of October. That meant that it was the first week of the new sales quarter. I did have my sales meetings which were more of building new deals because first, I was new and I had to build my own sales pipeline, and secondly if someone did not buy from me by the end of September knowing well that it was the end of our sales quarter which is the time when we are the most malleable and ready to give the most discount, there was little chance that that someone would buy from me in October where our company could afford to dig it's heels. Despite knowing this, the managers' job is to still nag the sales folks about deals they call "spill overs' and their quick closure, and it is the sales folks' role to endure such follow ups and look like ingenuous fools (while uttering facetious reasons on why the deals weren't closing), which the managers too were just until a few years back. In my experience, sales happen when they have to happen like everything in nature where, you cannot plan the time for the Sun to rise but plan the time of your waking up early to see the Sun rise, and similarly, you cannot plan when the deal will close but be ready to close it when the right time comes, and therefore, I find all sales forecasting meetings to be compulsive yet meaningless endeavours by the sophisticated workers of the company who, instead of predicting when they will be ready for the deal, try to predict when the customer will be ready.

My manager called for the sales forecasting meeting on Friday, asked the Mumbai sales team to not plan any client meetings on that day, the meeting was from 10 AM to 5 PM, after which, we were to go to Café Mondegar in Colaba for some beers. No client meetings meant no Lucky and so, I took another taxi from Chheda Nagar to my office in Bandra-Kurla Complex. I reached in time, but in my effort to beat the morning rush by leaving early, I did not have breakfast at home, and then I had a couple of toasts with a masala omelette after a plate of poori bhaaji in our small office cafeteria. After the breakfast, I still had about 20 minutes with me, and I thought of going through my presentation once more, which I couldn't because as I was about to leave the cafeteria, my colleagues walked in, who, on knowing that I wanted to go through my presentation once again, did not let me leave after teasing me for what I wanted to do, and so we sat in the cafeteria again where some of them ate their breakfast, and all of us had tea.

The meeting was super fun, like it always is, where stories are spun by every presenter who, having missed his sales target by miles in the last quarter, shows a sales pipeline from which orders worth millions of dollars would come out in the new quarter. Holes are blown through these stories by the managers, which is all fun to watch with surreptitious chuckles, but for that hour when it is your turn to get roasted. But this meeting had a surprise that was revealed in the end. We had four sales teams – North, South, East, and West. We were part of the West team. The team achieving the highest sales was to get a 'three days', all expenses paid vacation in Las Vegas, and the team coming second would be going to Thailand. This was more than good to excite all of us, and since the meeting ended with this announcement, all of us were more than eager to start for Café Mondegar as soon as we could, hoping to find easily, without having to wait, a table to seat the six of us (including our manager) on that Friday evening. We hailed a taxi in which three of us sat, including me, and the other two, we convinced them to come with our manager in his chauffer driven car. As soon as our ride started, Mahesh, my colleague, who was sitting in the front passenger seat, turned in his seat and said "Boss, we need to come second. In Las Vegas, we can attend a conference any time. The real fun will be in Thailand. Also, this will be the first time when I will be able to tell my wife that I am going to Thailand and not worry about it", before he winked, brought his palms together in a clap and started to rub them, perhaps to warm his hands to grab the opportunity. "Sahi hai", my other colleague Vivek chipped in. "An all-men trip has to be to Thailand only, and not to Las Vegas", he said before looking at me and adding "Bhai, sandwich massage lenge roz". Just as some more vivid descriptions of the sandwich massage started to be discussed, our taxi driver, who was an old man, shifted a little in his seat, and this made us a bit conscious because even though we were in our primal elements then, we were still behind the veneer of decency in our formal attires with tie and all, which was incongruent with the priapic spirit of our discussion. So, we shifted our conversation to more acceptable topics like the going property rates, stock market, and such which are engaging topics too because for people like us, they hold the hope of becoming rich, and in such a hope, the killing traffic too becomes bearable. We reached Café Mondegar in about an hour - at around six.

Café Mondegar is one of those must do places that every city has which, when they come in existence, are ahead of their time, cater to the suave and the bohemians more regularly, and the wannabes in between, but for which, time stands still while the rest of the city starts to move ahead and grows inexorably around them, and in the many ensuing years, such places age gracefully, are still known and frequented despite the newer and better places, more for the romantic old world charm that the old and the young like equally - the old for their congruity with their bygone time and the young for the incongruity with the present. I was very happy to be there in the way one is on seeing a landmark. On entering it, I found its size to be way smaller than its fame, the tables were too close to each other such that if one pulled a chair around one table, it would touch a chair or someone around another table, some tables were already taken, young, middle aged, old – all kinds of patrons were there, in groups or as couples, the waiters were moving around doing their job in their red t-shirts that had sky-blue sleeves and collars while faces from the murals on the walls were all gay and merry. In all, the setting was coming up slowly for a Friday evening. Luckily, a big enough table was available to us right near the entrance. We took it. Mahesh called one of our colleagues who were traveling with our manager and learnt that they were about twenty minutes behind us. We ordered our beers and some snacks and started the party.

We had our first pints very fast. The onion rings and fried calamari that we had ordered, came when the second pints were half way through and by this time, the others too reached, and joined us. Since I was new to the team, I was mostly silent. The rest were having a good conversation touching upon some funny incidents from their collective past about which I was oblivious, and hence, I was enjoying my beer and snacks, laughing with them when something funny was said, and answering any questions like "so, how do you find Mumbai?", when they were put to me. Our manager stayed with us for an hour, by which time, he had two pints of beer, some prawns and fish in snacks, and took our leave after telling Mahesh to pay for the party and claim it as reimbursement. Now that the cat had left, the mice were happy to play. The topic once again shifted to Thailand and the synchronized effort needed to come second.

I too was enjoying the conversation but with some nervousness because there was the mix of titillation at the thought of the sandwich massage and the guilt of the prig which, I know, is hypocrisy but then the sandwich massage is a thing that doesn't leave the mind

Every Day is Another Day

so easily. It was now nearly 8 PM and I wanted to leave. I told my friends that I had to head back home because the missus was alone with two small children, and even though I was already too late to do anything for her then, the least I could do was to not wake her up too late in the night. My friends had elaborate plans that involved having some more beer, go to Leopold after that to have some more beer, and then have dinner much later at Bade Miyan. They did insist but not too much because I was not yet a close friend. "You do this. Take a taxi from here to CST. From there, you take a harbour line train to Chembur. That is the fastest you will reach home", Mahesh said. "I have never been in a Mumbai local yaar. I have only heard that they are very crowded", I said. "Abe yaar, you are not at all a Mumbaikar if you haven't travelled by the local. And, at this time, there won't be any rush", he said, which I believed, took my leave, hailed a taxi, reached CST (Chhatrapati Shivaji Maharaj Terminus) in about fifteen minutes. When I got down from the Taxi, the massive grey edifice, which was built and opened by the British in the year 1887, stood before me in its majestic form. For a moment, I absorbed its sight. There was quite a hubbub. People were moving all around me, and there were too many of them. I regretted taking Mashesh's advice but by now, I was well into the course I had chosen and a bit hesitant in changing it by turning around and hailing another taxi to Chembur. I gripped my bag tightly and walked up the long and broad steps that took me inside the station. Large fans were circulating air in the large entryway. I stood inside with a mix of excitement, dithering, and eagerness. My feet were fixed to the floor, and my eyes were looking up at the high vaulted ceiling until I was shoulder pushed by someone from among the so many who were moving about me, and I heard "Aye, chal na" from somewhere ahead of me where there was only scurrying humanity. In my out of bearing stagger, I noticed the ticket counters to my right, to which, I waded through before standing in one of the long ticket queues. After ten minutes, I bought my ticket through a small hole in the window grill.

I reached home close to 10 PM, which is what, perhaps it would have taken me by a taxi because, people who travel by train and who extoll its virtue of being the quickest travel option, conveniently fail to mention the time needed to reach the station, if without a monthly pass, the time to buy the ticket, the waiting time for the train to come, the jostle to somehow get inside it, get thrown out at the destination station, and then the time needed to reach wherever one has to finally reach by a taxi, autorickshaw, bus or, by taking the humble walk. When the missus opened the door, she took my laptop bag, I entered the house with my shoes on, and sat on the sofa. The missus rushed inside and got me a glass of water, which I drank. Standing close by, she asked "what happened? You look so hassled". I just gave her a resigned look of the kind that begets sympathy. She sat next to me, put her hand on my shoulder, and asked "was work load too much today?". I shook my head in denial to which she asked "then what happened?". I said "I had sandwich massage", which the missus did not know what it actually was, and said "accha, having fun all by yourself when I am struggling at home with two small children. Now, tell me where you had the massage, and did you bathe or not afterwards?". I wanted to know if she had had dinner, she said "yes", I asked about the children, she said "they are sleeping", I brought down her hand from my shoulder, held it between my palms, and said "alright, let me tell you about the sandwich massage".

"Do you really not know about the sandwich massage?", I asked with a show of incredulity. The missus shook her head in denial. I explained vividly out of my own imagination. The missus was amused but she said "Chhee", punched me on my shoulder, and said "If that is what you have done, don't even come near me", in the playful way of an Indian missus where her belief in the husband's fidelity is not shaken by the husband's own claims of wavering because if not often, at least once, every Indian missus is known to say "I somehow agreed to marry you otherwise, you would not have got anyone".

I recounted my harrowing experience in the local train, vividly explained how at every station, more people boarded the compartment than the ones who alighted, that how, with every entry and egress, people would squeeze past me as though I was something to be juiced, that I had to keep myself straight and elongated and keep my nose above the heads to catch whatever was left of the warm air to avoid the bitter sweet smell of perspiration all around me when I could feel my own sweat trickling down my back and my sides, and then when Kurla came, how, instead of a sandwich until then, people surrounded me on all sides so tightly, that I had become more of a stuffing inside a roll. Finally, at Chembur, I could get down only because as the train moved from Kurla, out of some hunch, I asked one of the faces that were too close to mine, "how many more stations to Chembur?", and taking the tone of an urgent advice, the gentleman told me to start moving towards the door if I wanted to get down. "Bhaisahab, Chunabhatti ayega,phir Tilak Nagar, phir Chembur. You start moving ahead", he said. Heeding the advice, I started to move which was a very deft manoeuvre not only on my part but also on the part of the so many people who, despite being tightly packed and literally sticking to each other, moved the bodies and limbs to make some way for me and the few others who too wanted to alight at Chembur.

"So, this is your sandwich massage?", the missus said before adding "who asked you to come by the local train?", to which I did not say anything. Looking at my straight face, the missus laughed and so did I, after her. "It is quite late already, let us go to bed", she said. She walked inside and came back quickly with a change of clothes for me. "Don't make too much noise, put your shirt and trousers on top of the washing machine, don't switch on the bedroom light when you come inside - the children will wake up", she said after passing on the lungi and the t-shirt she had got for me, and then returned to the bedroom. I kept the clothes by my side on the sofa where, until a few moments ago, the missus was sitting, then very slowly and softly, without making any screeching sounds, I pulled the teapoy closer to me, sat back on the sofa, and rested my legs on top of the teapoy. I leaned my head backwards and stretched out. Now that the vigour of recounting my 'sandwich massage' experience had ebbed, the alcohol, which was still inside me, but which was in a moderate dose, instead of pushing me to crash in bed, pushed a philosophical spark up, and I thought "Aah! There is no place as comfortable as home", is how most of us, if not all, exclaim, as soon as we plonk on our couch or on our bed after returning from that vacation for which first, we long, then plan, then temporize with cavils, and then eventually take it for what we, the salves to earning a livelihood, believe, an impermanent manumission. A glutton who gorges all kinds of delicious food, when asked to rate the best food, will, with a good chance, rate the simple food of home as the best. Similarly, the favourite raiment that makes one look suave, as soon as one returns home, is first loosened by unfastening the hooks or the buttons to let one breathe before eventually being put back on the peg or on the hanger or being thrown in the laundry basket to get into the comfort of the pyjamas. We may go far and wide in search of all the things we covet but keep longing for home perhaps because even when we don't know it to be so, what we hanker for is mostly closer to home which, like someone holding a book too close, we can't see." In the matter of massage, men are sinfully rapturous about looking away from home for a typical massage they call 'the sandwich massage' so much so that they can lie to their wives about their destination or, do quirky things like working hard to come second in the team sales contest to get to go to Thailand instead of to Las Vegas which was for the winning team. However, for me, the ineluctable pleasures of the sandwich massage, although devoid of its lubricious intents, were available closer: at home. Therefore, my vote shifted from coming second to coming first, which of course, was a matter out of my control.

We came third in the sales contest. The team from North came first because they bagged a big government order which was a spilt over deal from the previous two quarters when finally, the tender was awarded. The team from South came second beating us by a thin margin.

The Bullet

That local train ride was the first and the last one for me for a long time to come, until which, I was back to my taxi rides. It was like one of those things one does in the heat of the moment or, under some intoxicating influence when the senses are dull, or rarely as a one off thing like many people in India who say "nahi ji, we are vegetarian, in our home, eggs too can't be brought", but they don't mind eating chicken and lamb in restaurants, but only when the meat is in neat shapes and sizes, its actual smell and taste is firmly obscured by the rich masala in which it is fried or roasted or cooked in a gravy, who leave their vegetarian way either under the influence of alcohol or by the goading of a friend who says "abe kha le, kuch nahi hota hai" with the same nonchalance with which Mahesh had goaded me to take the local train.

Anyway, the days passed. In a few days, it was now two years in Mumbai. How else to put it when time passes so fast that that on looking back, a day in the distant past appears as though it was yesterday. Our girl was now in pre-kindergarten and our boy was in what they call a playschool in the same place at Rajawadi in Ghatkopar which is a suburb, one can say, abutting Chheda Nagar. The children had started to pick words and phrases in Gujrati, and Khakhra was now an ever-present snack in our home, and the missus had already marked the place from where, in that winter, for the first time in our lives, we were to get a special Gujrati mixed vegetable called Undhiyo. Without our feeling it, Mumbai was growing on us, and with a passing understanding of Marathi, a bit of Gujrati also brushed on us.

That November, which was also the Diwali month, I bought

Every Day is Another Day

my Bullet Classic 350 Cc motor cycle which is right at the top of happiness giving things to middle class males, the other fantasy being a jeep which, even though coveted more, costs more and continues to remain a fantasy for most, unlike the Bullet, which can be had. Now, this Bullet is a very macho thing with its bulk, and unlike the vroom vroom of the race bikes, its engine gives heavy thuds which makes the men go crazy. It is not so much that I bought the Bullet, the important thing is that I got to buy it. Despite my non-macho domesticated life, my body with a bulging waistline, protruding belly, receding hairline, a large pair of spectacles, loose baggy trousers, and full sleeve shirts, I could own a brand-new Bullet. This is important because in it lies the mantra of keeping the human society in general order where even the undeserving get to enjoy a bit so as not to have pent up frustration. If the pleasures one does not deserve are not had, the pent-up frustration will find vents to release the tension, and this will come in the way of society's tranquillity. If this were not so, so many men wouldn't even get to marry and have sanctioned physical intimacy because, unlike the animal world where only the alpha males get the females and the best among other things, and the rest are left with wounded pride that they try to forget by frolicking or fighting, alpha males in the human society are put in check by the system of work, wages, family, and mortgage so that others too could have a go at life frolicking, but without fighting.

Normally, for Diwali, we would have gone to our home town Ranchi but that year, my parents were away in the US visiting my younger brother. For Diwali, which was on the 9th of November, we went to Pune on the morning of 8th and returned on the evening of 10th because my in-laws couldn't have it that we spent the Diwali alone in Mumbai. Putting aside the sentiment of taking delivery of the motor cycle on the Diwali day, I brought home my new bike on the 4th which was just the next day of our marriage anniversary. I wanted the bike to be the gift to us on the anniversary but the 3rd was a Saturday, and it is considered inauspicious to buy any 'made of iron' stuff on a Saturday. For the anniversary dinner, I wanted to take the family out on the bike but that couldn't happen, and finally, we went to the first-floor restaurant of 'The Jewel of Chembur' by an Autorickshaw.

The missus was as such indifferent to the idea of the bike. When I did bring it home the next day late afternoon at around five from the Royal Enfield dealership at Bhandup, she did welcome the motorcycle with an aarti and a small pooja, and put a vermilion dot right in the middle of the headlight and on top of it. That's it. Only my daughter was enthused about the bike and wanted a ride at once. When I picked up my daughter and put her astride in front of me such that she was sitting on the petrol tank on not on the seat, from somewhere behind me, Ganesh came running shouting 'uncle, uncle', quickly jumped onto the rear seat and held me tight with his hands extending as far as they could around my middle, and said ' mai bhi round lagaunga'. We went a couple of times around Chheda Nagar along the long road that circumscribes it like a ring road.

I did not feel the otherwise tedium of Monday because I was quite excited about my bike ride to the office. It was already the holiday season and there was neither much work load nor any important customer meetings. There wasn't the need to call Lucky. I got ready to leave home by eight thirty in the morning. I had bought a new helmet from the bike dealership before I took delivery of my bike. With my laptop bag slung across my shoulder, I picked up my helmet, tucked my mobile phone inside the right pocket of my trouser, and from beside the TV, I picked up the two keys of my bike

– one for the ignition and one to unlock and turn the fuel knob. I said goodbye to the missus, kissed my baby boy on his cheek who was moving about in his blue half pants and yellow t-shirt which were his uniform, tapped my girl on her head, who was busy playing in the living room with a steel bowl and a spoon, and stepped out. When I reached near my bike, though it was still shining clean, some dust had settled on the seat and the petrol tank. I walked back and knocked on the door which, the missus opened. "Did you forget something?", she asked on seeing me. "Is there some small cotton cloth that I can use to clean the bike?", I asked her. "One minute, let me see", she said and walked back inside. She came back quickly with an old white handkerchief of mine and asked if that would be okay. "Yes", I said, took it from her and turned back. When I reached by bike again, in the brief interregnum, avian discharge was splashed on top of the head lamp and near the odometer. I felt utterly disgusted. I looked to my side from near the bike and I saw the missus standing near the open slide, looking at me from the living room. I pointed my finger at the head lamp and asked her for some water. She once again went inside and brought some water in a glass tumbler that she passed on to me through the grill. I poured all of it on top of the head lamp and since the bird shit was still wet and not sticking obstinately to its place like it does when it dries, all but a few specks of it flowed down with the water. With the old handkerchief that I was clutching tightly in my hand in frustration, of which I was not conscious, I wiped clean my bike starting with the head lamp, going over the seat, and finally the front mudguard, having run out of patience to wipe the number plate in the rear and the tail of the rear mud guard sticking out from under it. When I was done, the handkerchief was soiled with greasy dirt. I kind of crumpled it in a ball and tucked it at the side of the bike in the gap between the air-filter box and the chassis frame. I then put on my helmet that I was holding all this while, sat astride my bike, pushed it off its stand, and then pushed it back to take it out. My laptop bag, which was slung across me with its strap going from the left shoulder, across my body, and then going over the right side of my waist, found its place on the seat but is started to lean backwards. I shortened the length of the strap using the plastic loop and then, it sat tight and straight against my back. It was now time for the starting ritual of the Bullet. With my right hand, I pushed out the kick pedal. Using the thumb of my left hand that was holding the handle bar, I pushed open the decompress lever and lightly pushed the kick, the way they taught me at the dealership, and the needle in the pressure gauge came right in the middle, which, until then, was leaning to the right. I stood up from the seat, my right foot was already on the kick pedal, I kicked it down lightly, the bike started with its deep base frequency laden thud thud, I opened the throttle, and the engine stopped. I tried again, going over the entire ritual. The bike started, and as soon as I opened the throttle, it stopped again. In exasperation, I sat down on the seat and brought down my hands from the handlebar, and slumped. " try slowly with some patience", I heard the missus say, who was still looking at me from across the grill, whose conviction about everything wrong with me is that I am impatient and I try to do everything too soon. Not having anything to lose, I heeded her advice and kicked again. As the thud thud started, I waited for a couple of seconds, and then, very slowly, rotated the accelerator. This time, the engine woke up nicely. I let go of the accelerator, slowly again, and the engine idled continuously. This brought relief to me. I looked to my right where the missus was. She didn't say anything but she had that smug look on her face: of getting it right once again. I waved my hand in goodbye, she waved back, and I left for my office.

The traffic on the road was comparatively less because of the

Every Day is Another Day

holiday week but a bit less in Mumbai is still quite much in the same way as a billionaire's thirty billion becomes twenty-five billion during a market correction in which he, of course becomes poorer by five billion, but he still remains quite rich. I rode easily on the wide express highway until Suman Nagar traffic signal where there was a long hold-up, as always. Until that day, I had crossed this place in Lucky's taxi, sitting at the back in its cool interior, protected from the heat, the dust, and the smoke outside. However, my bike could offer no such protection to me, and I kept waiting for the signal to turn green, which of course I couldn't see from far behind where I was, in between the so many cars, buses, trucks, other scooters and motorcycles, inhaling the stinking and smoke-filled air, and just then, the car to my left inched a bit forward because some space opened up, the city bus behind it moved forward and stood right beside me such that my front tyre was in line with its rear wheel arch from the front of which, I could see its exhaust pipe, when its driver, perhaps flustered by the wait, revved its engine, and dark smoke came billowing out of that exhaust pipe. I held my breath but I couldn't hold it for more than a few seconds, and when I inhaled, I almost fainted. But just then, the traffic moved forward and goaded by the incessant honking from all the sides, I too moved forward. But a similar torture awaited me ahead under the Sion bridge where I had to take right, where once again, I had to wait in traffic. Having then endured the Sion-Dharavi stretch of the road, and a brief hold up again before one took another right towards the Western Express Highway, I reached my office in Bandra-Kurla Complex around thirty minutes past nine. When I finally switched off my bike, still straddling it, I could feel the heat from its engine radiating out. I parked it, pulled out both its keys, put them inside my pocket, and went to my office where, after I placed my helmet and my laptop bag at my desk, I had to go to the washroom to wash my face, which had a hassled look.

In the evening, I could leave office only around seven O'clock which was peak rush hour.

Enduring the traffic woes, the dust and the smoke, and loud honking all around, after a long time since I started from office, I, on my Bullet, got into Chheda Nagar. Though I thought that I was almost home now, my woes still continued.

Chheda Nagar always has a deserted look. It cannot be used as a thoroughfare which makes vehicular traffic very sparse, and unlike any other residential locality in Mumbai which is self-sufficient with shops, restaurants, fuel pumps, garages, clinics, hospitals, Chheda Nagar has only residences and that too as three or four storeyed buildings. When such a thing happens, while the people get used to their peace, so do the street dogs. I entered Chheda Nagar and continued my ride along the longer stretch of the inside road. There were hardly any people there but for a bunch of men huddled outside the small paan shop close to where one enters Chheda Nagar from the service road, just about two or three old people were ambling slowly, perhaps towards the temple, and under the light of the dim street lamps and the headlight of my bike, I was able to see three dogs lying idly on the right side of the road. As I continued my slow ride, one of the dogs stood up with its tail straight, while the other two remained as they were. I was closely watching the dogs. As I drew close to them, the one that had stood up, started to walk diagonally across the road towards me. As it happens, in such cases, more than one's senses, one is carried onwards by the momentum of what one is doing and so, I kept on riding at the slow speed that I was in. The dog continued coming towards me with its head extended out, its body straight along its spine, its tail lifted up and straight, and with its gaze holding mine. I was in the middle of the road. I veered my bike towards the left to make some distance between us. The dog stopped in its advance as I neared it but just as I moved ahead of it, with a loud growling sound, it charged at me from behind. I turned back my head instantly and I could see that it had already caught on me. There was hardly any distance between its open mouth the inside of which, I was able to see even in the dim light because my eyes were wide open with horror. In my utter panic, I hit on the brake pedal with all my weight and my bike stopped with a screech and its rear tyre skidded towards the right. Reflexively, my left foot came off the brake pedal and I was able to stop the tilt of my bike and somehow, break its fall along with mine. The moment my bike stopped, the dog stopped in its track, turned, and ran back to its friends who, by then, were sitting up and looking at the commotion. Now, all the three started to bark loudly. I caught my breath while feeling my heart racing inside me. I continued to look back at the dogs and then at the road behind me. The few people who were walking had stopped in their place, but now, slowly started to take their steps forward. My bike was still idling. I looked to my side. From the first-floor grilled balcony of the apartment block close to me, a middle-aged woman and her teenaged daughter were looking at me, with smirks on their faces. Insult is felt after every injury. Thus, laden with both, the insult and the injury, I put the bike in gear, and slowly moved forward, but still turning my head back after every little distance forward to be sure that the attack did not resume. It did not. I reached home shortly thereafter. Perhaps from the sound of the bike, the missus made out that I was back because, as I entered my apartment block, the missus opened the door. "How was the bike ride?", she asked, even before I entered. "Good", I said. Once inside, while the missus was closing the door, I supported myself against the back of the sofa to take off my shoes. The right one came off nicely. As I put my right foot down and folded the left one, I noticed that shoe's sole had slightly come off at the heel. The missus too noticed it. "How did your shoe get torn?", she wanted to know. "I don't know, I did not notice until now", I said. After the missus let go of the matter and went inside, I sat on the sofa and thought whether it, that is my bike, was the right gift by me to myself for my anniversary and also for Diwali.

Years earlier, in one of our MBA classes, the marketing professor had taught us about post purchase cognitive dissonance. I had understood it well then. But on that day, after the harrowing time I had with my motorcycle, about the PPCD concept, I was enlightened.

Anyway...

New trousers at Raymond's

Diwali went very well in Pune. We returned to Mumbai the very next day.

The day after my first motorcycle ride to office, I hired the services of Ajay, who, when I woke up on that day and stood by the open shutter of the living room having my coffee, I noticed, was cleaning a car. I finished my coffee, put on my slippers, came out of my apartment, and walked up to him. When I reached him, Ajay was just straightening after dipping a maroon cotton cloth in the orange water bucket that was next to him, and squeezing out the excess water back in the bucket. " Bhaiyya, will you clean that motorcycle also every day?", I asked him pointing towards my Bullet. "Haan Sahab, kar denge", he said. When I asked him "how much?", he asked for one fifty rupees per month, to which I agreed. Therefore, when I walked out of my apartment on the Monday after returning from Pune, all I had to do was start my bike and go to the office. I was wearing my new cotton trousers that I had bought for Diwali. It was the right size when I had bought it sometime late in September when the discount season was on before the fresh stock for Diwali comes. When I had worn the trouser on the evening of Diwali, I had felt it a bit tight at the waist. When I wore it on Monday morning, it felt even tighter. When the bike started to move and I pulled my left leg up too, I could feel my stomach squeeze against the band of the trouser around my waist. But that must have been because of the last few days of eating, I thought. Soon after reaching my in-laws' place, I figured out that my mother-in-law had already made rava laddoo, chakli, gujia, chivda, fried maida diamond biscuits from what the mother and the daughter were discussing sitting at the dining table while I was talking to my father-in-law. These sweets and savouries were in large steel containers which were full when we reached there but which were left with only the last crumbs by the time we left. On the Diwali day, now that the combined forces of the daughter and the mother were at play, they made besan laddoo, mysore pak, and coconut barfi adding to the already long list of sweets. I was the one who had to eat the first of all these new sweets to let the ladies know how they had come out. In between, my father-in-law, late in the morning, took out his Honda Activa around eleven and got Shrikhand and Aamba Barfi from Chitale Bandhu.

In the office, my discomfiture persisted. First, I thought I should loosen my waist belt but that was already loose because the buckle was dangling below the trousers' button. The trouser was sticking to my waist tightly. Thereafter, every now and then, I would get up from my chair, tuck my fingers inside the waist band, and move them around in the hope that that would loosen the trouser. Nothing helped. But then, I executed an ingenious idea that sprung up in my head. I went to the men's room, loosened the trouser by unfastening the button, pulled my tucked in shirt a bit out in the front such that it hung over the waist band a bit, and concealed the little gap in it behind the buckle. I was able to breathe better.

In the evening, I came home riding my bike with my trouser in the same obscurely unbuttoned way. But this time, instead of turning left from near the pan shop, I continued straight and used the inside lanes to reach home in order to avoid those dogs, that might still be there, of which I wasn't sure, but that, I was not keen on finding out.

After reaching home, when it was time to change my clothes, I took out my belt first and threw it on the bed. Still not having come to terms with the thing that the trouser that had fitted me well just a month and a half back should become so tight, I sucked in

Every Day is Another Day

my stomach and buttoned the trouser. I was in front of the mirror fixed to the wardrobe door. I exhaled and stood there scrutinizing myself. As I was still coming to terms with this fact that I wanted to deny, something shot out and hit the mirror so fast that I could notice only the thing flying back and falling on the bed behind me as the reflection of its trajectory in the mirror. Instinctively, I turned back. It was the button of my trouser. I turned straight again while feeling the broken sewing that was holding the button in its place until then. This was too much. I hastily came out of the room and found the missus in the kitchen. Standing at its door, with my hand holding the door frame in the same way as Gurdutt's silhouette stood in Pyaasa, I asked her if I had put on weight. The missus looked at me with a turn of her head and said "yes, a little bit".

In the night, when I came to bed, the missus was lying on her side, turned away from me facing the children who were fast asleep. I thought the missus was sleeping too. I sat on my side of the bed with my feet on the floor and my palms pressing the bed. "What happened? Not getting sleep?", the missus' voice came from behind me. I turned. She was half lifted on her elbow with her face turned towards me. "No, not that. I was just thinking about my gaining this weight", I said while moving my right palm around my stomach, feeling it and then pressing the flabs on my sides. "I think I should start dieting", I said. The missus sat up on hearing this. 'No, no. You will become weak. Just stop eating outside. Nothing bad happens with home cooked food. And then, you don't do any physical activities also na. Why don't you start going for morning walks?", the missus suggested. She said the thing that I wanted to hear because the idea of dieting, even though my own, was atrocious. Walking sounded like a better option, and I promptly said "yes, yes, from tomorrow, I will start. You wake me up at six". I then pulled up my legs and stretched on the bed.

The missus shook me up exactly at six. This was an hour sooner than my normal waking time. While I was still in deep sleep from which I was being pulled out, as soon as my sleep broke, without any lingering, I sat up because like all new things, even the idea of morning walk was exciting because of its novelty. It took me half an hour to get ready for my walk. I was already in my shorts and round neck t-shirt in which I had slept. I had a pair of Reebok sports shoes that I was using as casual wear, which on that day and a few more days thereafter, got used for its meaningful purpose. I came out of our apartment block at around thirty minutes past six. Next to the Murugan temple, there is fenced walking track around a raised mud filled playground in which, people play cricket in the morning. I came to this place and started my morning walk among a good number of people who were doing the same and an odd one or two who were jogging. I did some five rounds and then sat on a low wall along the fence, feeling nice in the weather that was pleasant, and the slight breeze that was there. After some time, I got up, and reached home. The time was seven. The missus liked what she saw. There was sweat on my brow and some of it was showing on my t-shirt as well. "Arre waah. You did half an hour of walking on the first day itself", she said. When credit was coming my way, there was no point in denying it even though I knew that I had actually walked for only fifteen minutes, I was sitting by the walking track for a good amount of time, and even though the weather was pleasant, it was pleasant by Mumbai standards, and fifteen minutes of walking was more than enough for perspiration to show in its ever-humid conditions. At breakfast, the missus insisted that I had an extra paratha because I had exercised, I too did not resist, because I was hungry.

The entire rest of the week, I went to work, including to my client meetings, in that ingeniously done yet obscurely unbuttoned

Every Day is Another Day

trousers of mine because by then, I realized that all my trousers had become tight. Saturday morning, at around ten, I told the missus that I needed to buy some new trousers and that I needed to go to the Chembur Market. After breakfast, I took out my motorcycle and came to the Raymonds showroom near Ambedkar Circle. Inside the showroom, as soon as I entered, an old and loyal to the establishment salesman – which was evident from his mannerisms, came to me, and asked "jee, kahiye Sir". "Pants dekhna tha", I said. "This side Sir", the sales man said and indicated to me to follow him towards the left side of the showroom where, trousers were stacked on shelves and hanging along a long steel rod below the shelves. "Formal pants Sir?", the salesman asked. I said "yes", and then added "dark shades only". The salesman took one long look at me from top to bottom and then started to look for the right trousers from among the ones that were hanging on the rod. "I said 36" size me nikalna". He stopped what he was doing, took a good look at me once again, put his hand inside his pocket, took out a rolled measuring tape, walked up to me, said " haath uthaiye", when I lifted my hands, looped the tape around my waist, measured it, went back to the trousers, took out a navy blue one, gave it to me, indicated towards the trial room which was behind the shelves, and said " try this and see". I took the trouser, and as I was walking towards the trial room, I noticed that on the tag, the size mentioned was 38". 36" to 38" inches – perhaps the missus was right in saying 'just a little bit'.

The new trouser fitted me well around the waist. Since the waist size was 38", proportionately, the legs were wider too and so, I felt that it was a bit loose in the thighs and a bit sagging at the back, which I mentioned to the salesman as my objections when I was looking at myself in the long mirror along a pillar in the showroom. The salesman moved from beside me to come and face me, again took one long look at me from top to bottom, came close, pulled the trousers up because I was wearing it low at the hip like heroines in Hindi movies wear their saris, walked back, looked at me again, and said "excellent fitting Sir".

I came back home at around noon with three new trousers after waiting for nearly half an hour at the showroom for them to adjust their lengths. And so, the days went by in my wearing the new trousers in the hope that my morning walks will eventually let me shed the extra kilos, in which case, I will once again get to wear my old trousers and also wear the new ones by altering them, which is a service, the salesman at Raymonds let me know that they provided. Because, like Makeup is a thing that makes a beautiful woman more beautiful but it can't do much for the simple ones, when a man is wide in the middle, even the best fitting clothes can't do much for him.

Only Two Rotis

It was now beyond mid-November, and I got very busy. We had only half of the quarter left to close all our deals. The efforts had to be doubled up because the last week of December is holiday season for the big guys who sign the orders because they go to places like Goa and all to celebrate the New Year's Eve. In this relentless pursuit of business, there were way too many meetings which led to way too many lunches and dinners with clients. Then there was stress too which comes from nagging phone calls which, I fail to understand because, each of the orders I was chasing was for like twenty lakh rupees or thereabout, which in USD terms in those days was just about fifty thousand dollars, when not any of these orders was even loose change for the multibillion corporation of which I was a 'one of the' type humble employee, my manager's focus was unwavering from me which was evident from the many phone calls and message that were coming from him because someone in Singapore had his unwavering focus on my manager because someone in Australia had his unwavering focus on the Singaporean because someone in the US had his unwavering focus on the Australian, and while all this focus was great, my customers were not at all bothered. They have something they call 'Process' which is the nicest way of saying 'I will do it later'. But somehow, going through the processes of all my clients, in the end, I was able to collect my last order on the 31st of December, finished my last call of the day from my manager while on my way home in Lucky's cab. For the party, there was home cooked paav-bhaji, and a small cake that the missus made at home. I did pick up some beers from Amar Mahal.

As the new year dawned, so did the next quarter. First of January was a holiday for us, but a phony one because on the second, corporate slaves like me had the quarter planning meeting for which, one had to prepare long spreadsheets and presentations on the first, which too were phony, and for all this trouble, like firing at a man who is already dead, the meeting went from morning till evening with something known as the working lunch for which, pizzas were ordered. This phony business did not end here. In between the meeting, after the pizzas and the colas were given and therefore had, when it was time for the tea and the biscuits to come, the lady from the human resources department knocked on the door, pushed it slightly open and peeped in, my manager nodded at her from his pushed-back position in the swivel office chair, she walked in, stood near the front of the conference room table, and let us know that they had organized a health check program on Friday, for which, all of us had to come. So, I did come. The health check camp was organized in our cafeteria. When I walked in through the door, all the tables and chairs had been put in a corner and the large, now vacant, space in the middle was where, around a long table, in white coats over their habiliments, two ladies were on the left side, and a rather young man and a lady were on the right. We were to go in one at a time. After entering the cafeteria, I hesitated for a moment without knowing which side of the table to go – to the right or to the left. Then, the young man called me forth, and as soon as I reached him, he checked my identity card, and then asked me to fill a form with my name, date of birth, phone number, and about any known health issues. After I filled the form, he showed me the weighing machine and asked me to get on it. Now, this weighing machine is next only to the mirror in speaking bitter raw truth, and this is why, the mirror is liked by beautiful people and the weighing machine is liked by slim people because every so often, the beautiful people like to be told that they are beautiful and

Every Day is Another Day

the slim people like to be told that they are slim which is so unlike the ugly and the fat who never want to be told the bitter raw truth. And so, I stepped on to the machine gingerly, after first taking off my shoes, placing my wallet and my watch on the table, so that the burden of the truth can be lessened, and as the scale rotated, I looked down to which, the young man said "please look straight", and so I did, without getting to look at where the needle was pointing, and then he said " 103", without saying anything further, and impulsively, I looked down, and gasped.

I stepped off the machine and followed the young man, who then made me sit in a chair that was there to his left. He then pulled the blood pressure apparatus on the table towards him, put the cuff around my arm, tightened it with the Velcro strap, and started to pump the rubber bulb to inflate the cuff. I felt tight in the arm. The young man started intently at the gauge, which was visible only to him. Then he turned a circular knob next to the bulb, a slight hissing sound came from the apparatus, he stopped turning the valve, my arm felt relaxed as the cuff deflated, he once again stared at the gauge intently, deflated the cuff completely, took the cuff out, and said "Sir, please wait outside for some time and come back after the next person behind you". I asked him "what happened?". He said "nothing Sir, just come back after some time. And sir, please feel relaxed". Another phony thing this was – creating a tense suspense and then asking me to relax.

I came out of the cafeteria. There were some five or six people already queued up. The person at the head of the queue walked in as soon as I stepped out and I stood in his place, after explaining to the person who was beginning to walk ahead that I have been asked to come back, to which, there was no protest. In about five minutes, the person who had walked in, walked out, and I entered again. This time, I went straight to the young man and sat in the chair. He once again put the cuff around my arm. After the thing was done, he said "Sir, your BP is slightly high. It is 140/90". I gasped again. "What does that mean?", I asked. "Nothing to worry Sir. This happens to a lot of people Sir. It is because of stress these days Sir. And, your weight is also high na Sir. You need to reduce at least ten kilograms Sir. Come Sir, we will take your blood sample. And Sir, please consult a cardiologist for the blood pressure". I tried to get up from my chair pressing against the arm rests because I was just told that I was sick, and I felt the terror of it, but the young man said "please keep sitting Sir", and so I sat back. One of the girls from the other side of the table got up, picked up a blood collection tube and a syringe and walked towards me.

Things had turned out to be too much. I just couldn't enjoy my lunch that day, even though I ate all the things in the veg thali that I took in our office complex's common canteen. I left for home early, at around five. At the Kala Nagar Signal, coming out of Bandra-Kurla Complex, I was waiting to take the left turn. I felt some itching in my right eye, and so I closed my eyes, and pushing my right index finger from behind my specs, as I started to rub my eyes, I saw the big round moustachioed face of Karthik. From that moment, I don't know how I reached home because I was reliving that day from many years ago, which happens on days like this when the mind takes a turn of its own, and the body, with a memory of its own, does things mechanically.

My mind went to that day about seven years ago, when I was still a rookie and in my first employment in Bengaluru, when on most days, some of us, including me, would keep hanging around in the office till late in the evening when most of the people would have already left for home. Of the people who would still be hanging around, most were of my ilk: early hires from campuses with the most recent ones under the tutelage of their seniors who were hired a year ago. Also, where we returned to from work were places where we stayed. They were not homes to which one longed to return as soon as one could after the day's work. Further, the nocturnal spirit of the youth needs no explanation. So, you can see, there was a long list of grand reasons for staying back in office till late in the evening.

On that fateful evening when again, some of us were in office when most had already left, I was not doing anything in particular. If anyone thinks that not doing anything is easy, I would say 'think again'. Not doing anything actually means that one does not know what to do which can come from either the decision paralysis induced by a wide choice of things to do or, from not having anything at all to do. If this were not enough, and to make it worse, this is the vacuum to where the devil rushes to make you do things that mostly have little gains and at times can be to your detriment by spawning tasks for the empty mind. As a direct consequence of this, I was multitasking between listening to some songs on my office computer, reading my personal emails and indulging in some conversation with anyone who would peep inside my cubicle. This could have continued unabated but for the intervention of nature that has somehow made sure that the languid eat more than the active and therefore, not only feel hunger more often but also are more sensitive to it. It was around nine already and suddenly, I was feeling very hungry. Normally, I would go home around this time with my two flat mates who were also colleagues. We had joined work here at around the same time. But these two were away – one on an official tour and the other for the wedding of his cousin. We had a cook who would come every evening to make dinner for the three of us. She had the key to the main door of the house. This is how it was for every bachelor accommodation in our days and I suspect it is the same even now because you can't be home when it is time for the cleaner or the cook to come, and the best way was to keep a key hidden somewhere in the trim of the door or under the pot or, give a key each to the providers of the services you were availing. On that day, I had asked the cook to not make any dinner. No, I could've comfortably eaten alone at home but the roomie who was attending his cousin's wedding, usually bought the veggies which, obviously he couldn't do while being away and there was none left in the fridge when I had checked it in the morning. He was to be back the next day.

The idea for me that day was to get home only when I was ready to crash in my bed. What is there in an empty dwelling to reach early? I had planned that before going home, I will eat something outside in a utilitarian way like a set meal or a small pizza. However, by the time in the evening of which I am speaking, my appetite was whetted greatly and I was craving for more than what I had originally thought. The thing I have come to realise of late is that it is not the lust for anything that reduces with age but what actually reduces is the ability of one to perform to the extent of the arousal. Twenty years ago, my lust for food that evening was such that I wanted to eat for dinner palak paneer, dal tadka, tandoori roti and to end it with some jeera rice topping it with the dal and eating each spoonful with a bite of roasted papad. But you can't order a portion each of all these when eating alone. You need someone to give you company and to partake in the sumptuous repast. Unlike the beginning of the weekend when generally there will be many enthused about going out for food and drinks, that day being a weekday, I had to really look for someone who would be ready, late in the evening, to eat with me. Our office was of four large symmetrical floors with each floor having two equal wings separated by a passage that also had a few cabins for senior managers and a couple of small meeting rooms. The stairs and the elevator shaft ran through one end of the passage such that one wing was abutting them and the other one was at the far end of the passage. I used to sit in the wing that was at the far end of the passage. I got up inside my cubicle to see if there was any other 'wanderer in office' who I could ask. I saw Kartik's large head popped on his big back. If there was a neck, it was not visible to the eye. Kartik was the gentle giant among us, the rookies. His overabundance could not be contained within the dimensions of the office chair the likes of which the rest of us used. He used a chair with no arm rests to let his flanks squeeze out unobstructed. I decided against shouting from where I was standing and I walked to his cubicle. "Kartik, what are you doing here still?", I asked. Like it happens, when a person utters words in a language different from his vernacular, elision happens, syllables shift or get added or get shunted completely, Kartik said, "Baiyya (When a South Indian says Bhaiyya, that is brother in Hindi), I just had some work to finish. Bas nikal raha hoon (I am just about to leave)".

"What are you doing for dinner?", I asked next.

Kartik explained that his plan was to call Shanti Sagar to pack his order that he would pick on his way home. Now, Shanti Sagar was a small restaurant at one corner of Bashyam Circle which was the intersection of Tank Road and 13th Cross, Sadashiva Nagar. It is not enough to just say Shanti Sagar in Bengaluru because there are so many of them and sometimes, a few of them are so close to each other that one needs to also specify the exact location to keep things clear. Already, 'Shanti' makes it a bit easier because of the so many restaurants in Bengaluru that have 'Sagar' suffixed to their names.

If one were to do a wild card search like *.Sagar, a list running into thousands will return. See, at the mere thought of Bengaluru, one comes up with metaphors related to the software industry.

Coming straight to the point, I said " I have also not eaten. Should we just go for dinner at Shanti Sagar? You leave after dinner".

I was pleased when Kartik said "Ok Baiyya". As an afterthought, he added "but you know, I am dieting. I don't eat more than two rotis these days".

"No problem at all! We will have some dal, sabzi and roti, and if you like, we can have a little rice later", I said to him in broad strokes without revealing my plan for the feast I had in mind.

Ok Baiyya.

I felt a bit contrite at my self-centredness to have stayed on the course of my focus to find someone to go with me for dinner and completely glossing over Kartik's point on his dieting. I quickly made amends by asking, with a show of concern, "but why are you dieting?".

Baiyya, I have to lose some weight. As though pre-empting the next question, Kartik added

"I can't exercise that much you know, walking or jogging. My knees pain. The doctor has also asked me to take it easy and control my eating first".

I got really concerned then. "Doctor! Why did you have to see a doctor?", I asked.

Baiyya, because of the bank guys. Sensing my bewilderment, Kartik quickly added "the bank guys suggested a life insurance policy to me. When I agreed, they filled the forms and then asked me to get my medical check-up done. I did. My blood pressure came out a bit high. So, I had to see the doctor."

Oh! I exclaimed with genuine concern. But you are alright right? No problem?

I am fine Baiyya.

What did the doctor say?

He said that it is because of my weight and that I should reduce it. That is why I am dieting and eating only two rotis these days.

Is there any medication?

Yes Baiyya.

And insurance?

They refused Baiyya.

I really did not know what to say to this. Finally, to put the matter to rest, I asked if we should go? "Chalo Baiyya" Kartik agreed readily.

We came down the couple of floors using the lift before stepping out of the building. Shanti Sagar was just around the corner and not even one kilometre from our office. I had suggested that we walked. It was not even ten minutes one way and then we could have come back after dinner. "Kartik, we can talk and we will get a good walk also", I had said.

No Baiyya. It will be late. I will go home directly from Shanti Sagar.

I looked at Kartik. He offered an innocent, round, big, spectacled and a thickly moustachioed face to which one could only have said yes. The face had equal proportion of expectancy and determination.

It was difficult to say whether Kartik was asking or telling. I acquiesced. Kartik asked me to hold his bag while he went to get his motor cycle from the parking

Soon, Kartik returned. "Baitho Baiyya (Brother, sit)", he said to me. I saw whatever was left of the seat behind Kartik. It was a very tight squeeze but I somehow managed to put myself on the bike with Kartik's bag pulled over my right shoulder, leaning a bit to my left so that I could look ahead over his shoulder and also speak to him while we rode.

No ride is short for a brief conversation. For young men who have not become dreary by maturing beyond their age, casual conversations with friends are either about girls or about drinks. I chose the latter line. "Kartik, I have some Rum at home. Why don't you come this Friday?", I offered. "I will come Baiyya", he said before surprising me again in a matter of just a few minutes by revealing that he now drank only beer. "You know Baiyya, I like rum mixed with coca cola. But coca cola is very sugary and it has a lot of calories. In leaving coca cola, I had to leave rum also. So, whenever I drink now, I just drink two bottles of beer", Kartik explained. Again, "hmmm" is all I was able to manage. Soon, we reached Shanti Sagar.

Right outside, we found a just enough slot between a scooter and a motor cycle that was put on its side stand. I got down to make it easy for Kartik to manoeuvre and fit in his motor cycle. However, it turned out that the space was not going to be sufficient and Kartik turned to me saying "Baiyya, thoda jaga banao na. (Bro, make some room please)". I went to the motor cycle on the side stand and straightened it before putting it on the vertical stand. A little bit more space opened up for Kartik to push his motor cycle in the slot while still sitting on it. When Kartik finally joined me, we entered Shanti Sagar that was not crowded at that hour on a week day. We took a table in the non-air-conditioned section close to the juice counter that was also accessible from the outside. No sooner we took our place than a boy came to wipe the table with a brown cloth that would have been white once. He wiped the table and in the next moment, put two steel tumblers with cold water in front of us. He then brought a couple of laminated menu cards printed front and back. This was unlike the booklet kind you got in the air-conditioned section but it still listed all the items under sections like Snacks, Main Course Indian, Main Course Chinese, Rice Items, Tandoori, Juices and Desserts.

I was very hungry when I had sought out Kartik but by the time it came for us to order our food, my craving had lessened. Right then, I was just hungry for some food, that was all. "Kartik, you decide what we will eat. I too don't feel like eating an elaborate meal. Order some sabzi, dal, and roti", I said to him.

Ok Baiyya.

Kartik scanned the menu card for a few minutes before looking up expectantly from side to side. This was the sign for the waiter designated to the table to come and take the order. The sign was picked up soon and a guy came with a notebook and a pen. He was dressed out of place in a cheap black suit. He came and stood next to us with his note book raised close to his chest with the tip of the pen already placed on it. Kartik looked up at him for just a moment and shifted back his attention to the menu card. "Baiyya, ek butter paneer masala, ek dal makhni, ek veg dum biriyani", he ordered. To me, he then turned to ask how many rotis I will be having. I said two. "Ok baiyya, get us four rotis", he finally confirmed to the waiter. "Sir, any snacks?", the waiter asked. "Baiyya, get two fresh lime sodas - sweet and salt mixed and two masala papads", Kartik added to our order.

"Get the masala papads and fresh lime soda first and fast", he added as an instruction. "Ok Sir", came another terse response from the waiter. He then finished noting our order, repeated it for our confirmation and left.

"Hey Kartik, that is lot of food. I can't eat all that", I said, though realising that it was already late for saying this.

"I will share na Baiyya", Kartik said to comfort me.

"But you said that you were dieting and you will eat only two rotis", I said.

"Yes Baiyya, rotis, I am eating two only".

I saw the innocent, round, big, spectacled and the thickly moustachioed face and went hmmm.

As I was entering Chheda Nagar, the blinding high beam from an oncoming car pulled me out of my reverie. Soon thereafter, I reached home. I did not reveal to the missus the events of the day but perhaps my face was revealing that not all was right with me. She asked "what happened? Why are you looking glum today?" I said "nothing, maybe, I am tired. And listen, I will eat only two rotis for dinner." The missus said "okay, I will make some rice too, I was anyway planning to make Kadhi. Kadhi chaval will be nice after rotis". I said "No, I will eat two rotis only. This walking shawking is not doing anything to me. I need to reduce weight. I will do dieting from today". The missus did not pursue the matter further, which was not her wont, because for everything, until she asks why, what for, who told you, and a few more in her usual line of catechism.

Well, at dinner, this is what happened. There were kadhi with pakodas, aloo-gobi subzee, rotis, boondi raita, and rice. I had to take my two rotis, the kadhi and the subzee on the side of my plate, and eat. But, after my two rotis, I just couldn't muster the will to get up because so far as food is concerned, satiety is more important than fulness. So, I scooped out a little bit of rice, put it in my plate, poured some kadhi on top of it along with one of the pakodas, took some more subzee, refilled my bowl with raita, and ate all of it.

So far as the blood pressure was concerned, I figured out soon enough that it was much easier to manage. I visited the cardiologist. He confirmed that my blood pressure was high. He was himself so wide in the middle that he did not suggest anything about reducing my weight. When I came out of his clinic, I had a small prescription. I just had to pop a small pill every morning.

PART 2

There comes a time when one is so overwhelmed by life that there is just no time to notice one's troubles as troubles. During this time, one sees one's children grow, one's career grows, and one makes more money because there are promotions and all. Therefore, the immediate learnings from troubles are suspended during these overwhelming and also happy years - which mostly last for about ten years after which, when your children stop listening to you, you once again become reflective. Now that I am on the wrong side of forty, trouble has started to visit me, though appearing at wide intervals because I have already learnt much, but in a very loquacious way such that it imparts its infrequent lessons more vehemently.

A decade is a long time. At the beginning of this decade, only small kids called me Ankal or Ankil, but by the end of it, teenagers were calling me the same. The missus, who was slim earlier, was now fuller, and her yearnings for silk and chiffon had given way to dress materials to get different fits of salvar kurta that she now preferred. By the end of this decade, we were a better match than earlier – Jha Ankal and Jha Anty. In the first half of this decade, my parents would come to Mumbai more frequently when the children were small because small kids are cute and all but for the grandparents, the pull of the grandchildren lasted only for about five years and they started to come less often asking us to come instead because they just couldn't adjust to the matchbox dimensions of my Mumbai home which people of Mumbai proudly call Two BHK. My in-laws too lessened their visits, but that is because my father-in-law found any kind of traveling, especially driving, even for a short distance like Pune-Mumbai, as tedious.

I stayed at Chheda Nagar until 2017 by when, I got possession of the apartment I had booked (on a loan of course) in Navi Mumbai, and we shifted there in the month of April. The children got admission in a good school and joined a good tuition centre as well (which you might find strange and say "why tuition classes when the school is good?", but I had to put them in tuition classes because I have to empower them and let them do whatever they are interested in so long as it is engineering), overall, life was good.

But before we moved in, there had to be a house warming ceremony. A new house of your own in Mumbai, even if it is in Navi Mumbai, is a big thing. My parents flew in and my in-laws came by an intercity cab. My in-laws had come earlier to help their daughter with the preparations. I had not yet vacated my Chheda Nagar home and the shifting was in the final stages. Before we started our move-in, we had got all the finishing work done which is a lot of ply work for the wardrobes, kitchen shelves, beds, and so many small things about which the contractor always says "will be done in two months", but actually takes more than six.

On the day of the house warming, all of us got up early to get ready on time given that we were six adults and two children with only two bathrooms available to us. I had my car and I had asked Lucky to come that day. All of us reached our new apartment complex by nine. Panditji was to come at ten.

My father was quite impressed with the complex as soon as he saw it. Behind the imposing entrance, there were high towers. Big things generally look good. Our building wing was close by from the entrance. The complex was a new one, and we were among the early ones who moved in. At the entrance, the security guard did not make much fuss about Lucky parking his car as well inside because many parking slots were as yet unallotted or vacant.

Taking the lift, which were two in each tower, we reached our new home. The missus took out the key bunch from her bag and opened the doors, and we all entered after taking off our footwear outside. The entire house was quite bright because the curtains had not yet come, and ample sunlight was coming in. The missus just switched on the fans. As with entering any new house, my parents and my in-laws were curious. They first looked about everywhere in the living room before walking up to the shutter behind which was the balcony. The missus and I had to see to some last-minute arrangements, and we got busy. There weren't going to be many guests but a couple of families of close friends but still, arrangements had to be made. So, we left the parents to see around.

After seeing around the house, my father and my father-in-law sat together on the sofa. The missus had made some chai in the meantime and brought it. While everybody was sipping their chai, I asked my father "how is the house?" "Its very nice, beta", he said with sincere emotion, made some space for my son, who just then came from somewhere inside eating a square piece of chikki, to sit beside him in between him and my father-in-law, and after taking another sip of the chai, as an afterthought, added "but it is a bit small". "Jha Sahab, in Mumbai, houses are like this only – just enough space. Most of the people live in one-bedroom houses. This is real luxury to have a 2BHK", my father-in-law said to my father, looking at him with his turned head. "That is true. In Mumbai, one measures a house by the number of rooms whereas in our place, we measure it by the number of floors. Whatever he has paid for this house, in Ranchi, we could have built a two-storey bungalow", my father added to which my father-in-law said "sahi baat hai". With this, the two retired folks got their topics for a protracted discussion on real estate prices, the builder politician nexus, corruption, and all which are from among the favourite subjects of pastime discussions because such discussions yield nothing other than killing the time. My son just got up and escaped inside while the phone call from Panditji rescued me. Panditji was at the gate, and he did not remember the wing and the flat number to make his entry at the security station. Panditji had come a bit early.

By three in the afternoon, everything was over. The housewarming pooja went well. My friends and their families had reached on time and they stayed throughout. Lunch, that I had arranged from a private caterer for about twenty people, was served inside the house at around thirty minutes past one. Just a few moments back, everybody else had left, and the eight of us remained, along with two gift boxes that my friends had brought. We returned to Chheda Nagar at around nine in the evening after first going to Chembur and having dinner at Gita Bhavan. The next day, my in-laws returned to Pune.

In the next few days, the rest of the work including the curtains was done, and on the last weekend of that month, we shifted. Swaminathan Maami was too old now. Our interaction was with Subbu only who would come every year to renew the lease agreement. Since we would pay our rent regularly and did not cause any trouble, Mami's younger son visited us only about a couple of times in all these years. I did invite them to the house warming ceremony but nobody came. Of the fifty thousand rupees I had paid as the security deposit ten years ago, I was to get back only twenty thousand because of the painting work Mami's son would have to do (after the last painting they did four years back) because of our leaving, and before leasing out the house again.

My parents stayed with us during this time and moved with us to the new house. The shifting was without much hassle. While they were there, our boy slept between his grandfather and grandmother in the children's room, and our girl slept in the living room on the couch.

The next weekend, my parents left for Ranchi. It was the beginning of May and the school was yet to resume. There weren't many people in the complex then and therefore, the children found it difficult to make new friends, and so, cycling inside the complex was their favourite pastime. The missus was deft at finding a helper soon for the household chores. My driving time to office extended by thirty to forty minutes but that was manageable. And in this way, we were now in our own house in Mumbai, paying as instalment a little more than the rent I was paying that had reached a sizeable amount with its five percent raise every year. The days started to move with their new rhythm but which became routine very soon.

The Missus and Her Simple Wishes

A few months had now passed. Surprisingly, quite a few people moved in in the month of May. This eased in June when by its 10th day, monsoon arrived with all its vigour. In the month of June, at least there would be a let off for a day or two but in July and August, it poured. Kharghar looked like a hill station. From our windows and the balconies, we could see the hills and faint silvery lines of waterfalls. On a Sunday in July, we planned to go to the waterfall. We got in my car and reached the golf course. With not much hassle, I found a place to park by the road side. We got down, and walked together, taking a lane to the left along the golf course, to go towards the Pandavkada falls. There was quite a crowd and many cars were parked on either side of the broken road that led us inside. Much before the falls, we found a jungle brook that was shallow but the flow of water was vigorous. In it, many people were sitting, lying, or standing, having fun. We also joined and spent some good time there. The children did not want to come out of the water. They were a bit further than where the missus and I were squatting in the middle, with the round smooth rocks and pebbles rolling beneath us and clean water flowing by our sides. After spending some time this way, I called out to our children. We came out of the water on the other side of the stream and started to walk towards the waterfall.

With some serious difficulty for me where I had to haul myself up some steep steps and then rocks, on somehow climbing which, I would extend my hand to pull the missus up whereas the children found all of this to be quite easy, we reached the waterfall. Here again, there was some serious crowd but with enough room to accommodate the four of us also among them, under the thundering water. With careful steps, we walked on the slippery rock to come and stand under the falling water. It hit my back like a whip but it felt nice. Our boy stood in front of me and this shielded him from the force. Our girl stood in between me and the missus, holding our hands tightly. At a moment not more than 20 seconds of our enjoying together like this, the missus, stepped out, leaving us where we were, from the pocket of her lower, pulled out her phone which was well wrapped in a polythene, took out her phone, found an obliging person, gave her phone to him and came back next to us. The person clicked a few pictures, and when he did the thumbs up, the missus once again stepped out, took her phone, saw the pictures in it, turned to look at us, clicked a few pictures of us, and then turned, lifted the phone up, and started clicking selfies.

The missus is a very picture taking person. She just keeps clicking - mostly selfies with her phone, or asks me or anybody to click anything nice with at least her being in the foreground. She is quite pretty, and many a head turn for her, but I believe she is a narcissist. We spent some fifteen minutes in and near the waterfall before walking back. Near the stream, at the only shack there, we had bhajia and vada-paav and finished it with hot tea. In two hours from when we left home, we were now heading back in our still wet clothes. Everyone was happy about this little escapade, especially the children. The missus turned in her seat and asked the children "maja aaya na", and they yelled out an emphatic "yes" and said for the first time "Papa, our new house is very good" because for their ingenuous minds, this new house was not only the apartment but also the hills, the stream, and the waterfall. Perhaps, an artless and innocent mind of a child is more expansive and joins together whereas a mature mind puts things in pieces and then the pieces as yours and mine. In this way and very soon, our new home accepted us completely and so did we. By the way, just a couple of days after our visit to Pandavkada, some serious mishap happened there, and the authorities restricted the entry of people in that area. It was some solid luck that we went there just at the right time. It kept on pouring for the rest of July and for most of August with some respite in September by the middle of which, the monsoon was retreating with some odd showers here and there. Without our realising, we had lived in our new house for five months already. In this time, we had made new acquaintances and friends in the complex.

September passed with Ganesh Chaturthi for which there was Ganesh Utsav in the complex, October passed with Nav Ratri for which there was Garba in the complex, and then came Diwali for which we went to Ranchi. This way, life was moving at a steady pace and then, some days after we were back, a day came, which was a Sunday, supposedly the best day of the week; the day for the coming of which, the rest of the days are endured. It is the best day because whereas the rest of the days dictate the pace and schedule of one's life, on a Sunday, one can set the pace and go about things in a leisurely way. The first thing to do generally, is to wake up much later than usual. Having said that, I would go on to say that 10 AM should be set as the limit for this allowance to not let one lose so much of the Sunday that its joys get mitigated. Anyway, as I lingered in my bed, light was filtering through the drape betraying that it was already much longer than usual. The air conditioner was turned off earlier but the chill still hung in the room. I was having my lie-in, half shrouded under the cover. "Get up, it's nine already", I heard the missus. I pandiculated, pushing the counterpane lower with my feet.

Still in my night shorts and vest, I ambled inside the living room. I was surprised that it was in a much better shape than how we had left it in the night. The center table that I had pulled closer to the sofa to rest my legs while watching TV, was in the center, the newspaper was on top of it, folded and crisp. The remote controls of the TV and the set top box were on the platform below our large LED TV. The cushions on the sofa were deftly arranged. It felt nice to be in a clean and well-arranged room. But, on a day, if the room is so clean that is it is cleaner than clean, in addition to the cleanliness, it could also mean either of these two things - that on that day, the missus is grouchy, and by cleaning and arranging things in the house, she is conveying how it is only she who cares about the house while bearing the indifference of its other inhabitants, or she is in a very happy disposition so much so that she does not know where to expend her vivacity, and from among the suitable alternatives, has chosen cleaning the living room. I found the missus at the kitchen island peeling peas. Kept close were some carrots, a large uncut potato, some florets of cauliflower. It appeared that the latter of the aforesaid held that day.

While continuing with that which was keeping her busy right then, she raised her lids and moved just her eyes to see that I had seen that she has seen me. "Coffee?" (We drink Coffee on Saturday and Sunday mornings, on the other days, we drink tea, there is no logic or rationale to this, just that this is how we are) she asked with a jerk of the head. I nodded. She removed the coaster from the top of a mug that was already on the kitchen platform. In the next moment, the microwave swallowed the mug and whirred for twenty seconds before making a shrill beep. Scalding hot coffee came out hiding the deceptive heat behind the missing froth. Coffee without froth is, imagine, like Jesus without his beard - both, still remaining what they are but not looking the part. The missus took another mug in her left hand and poured the coffee in it in a long thin squirt from the mug in her right hand that was raised higher. Swoosh. Then, the left hand went up and the right came down and the coffee was back in the first mug. The missus handed the mug to me in which, the coffee was as hot as it should be, and frothing. I took the first sip. The caffeine and the sugar instantly made me feel awake and not just out of my bed. I walked to the couch and slouched, drinking my coffee and reading the headlines.

"Get some Boondi", the missus tried to inveigle. "I will make Raita with Pulao. Okay?", she added.

I was engrossed in the newspaper, and I did not answer. "Are you listening?", the missus asked with irritation she was unable to hide. "Okay", I acknowledged.

"Get the Dahi that comes in plastic pouch. The one that comes in tub is too thick to make raita"

"You need it now?"

"No, get it any time before lunch"

I went about my coffee and the newspaper. When I finished, it was already half an hour since I had woken up, and I had not yet done the so many things that one has to normally do after getting up. It seemed to me that I was already late for my visit to the swimming pool in our apartment complex. When late to our swimming pool, one would find it to be under siege by the many children, their overseeing mothers who would be strolling by the perimeter pool gutter, and since they can't drown in the barely five feet depth of the pool, many water splashers. I got up to finish my morning routine. Finally, close to 10 AM, I got ready to go, and carrying the change of clothes, towel, swimming cap, swimming goggles, and shower gel, I reached the swimming pool. Surprisingly, there weren't many vying for aquatic pleasure on that day. I quickly walked up to the row of showers and put up a perfunctory act of cleaning myself before plunging in the pool.

After completing two slow laps, I relaxed by the corner of the pool bobbing in the water, supported by my extended hands that rested along the lip of the inner gutter. There were a couple of swimmers who were swimming vigorously. In my relaxed state, I just watched them unaffectedly. After every four laps they would stop at one end of the pool, huffing and puffing, and after a minute or so, would start again. They were in much better shape than I. Vigorous swimming can enhance one's quality of life in many aspects but who cared. I was behind quantity. In nature, the very active and flexible feline species may have more grace but it is the rotund and the slothful that are known to live longer, and therefore, are more likely to enjoy life and its vagaries. In my lazy indulgence, I spent more than an hour in the pool.

After the shower and the change of clothes, as I came out of the changing room and entered the hall where the table tennis and pool tables are kept, I saw a couple of my friends entering the hall from the other side which was also the exit for me. Now, when gentlemen meet, on purpose or by chance, after the initial courtesies, a bit about a few matters from among geo politics, sports, global warming, state of the economy, and such get touched upon, leaving lesser matters to the uncouth. By the time our conference got over, I noticed that I had been away from home for nearly two hours.

When I came back home, it was close to but already beyond noon. As I entered the house, after opening the door for me, my boy went back to the sofa from where, his elder sister was already watching TV.

My appetite was whetted to its extreme as it was only a cup of coffee that I had had since morning. What made the matter worse was the time spent in the swimming pool. Generally, anything on fire can be dipped in water to douse and cool it. However, for terrestrial beings, long time spent in water works the other way because it kindles the fire in the belly. As soon as she saw me, standing behind the island in our open kitchen, she said "Pulao is almost ready". I looked at the pressure cooker on the gas stove with its whistle already fidgeting so much that at any moment, it would have jumped with a shrill Shhhhhhhh. "See, they are watching TV since getting up so late. Ask them to go and have their bath", the missus said. I looked at my children and told them "go, do as your mummy says". They continued to watch TV. Just then, the missus stormed towards us, yelled at the children, who quickly switched off the TV and walked inside, then she stared at me, shook her head, said "can't even control the children", and walked away. I stayed in my place for a few seconds thinking if this was all it had to take to get the children to bathe, why couldn't she have done it before but then, the missus, who was still upset, while still near the kitchen platform, said "every time, I only need to shout and then become bad to my children, and you will always remain good". I stayed quiet. "Get the Dahi fast", she said.

I unburdened my bag by first putting my swimming trunk and the wet towel in the basket by the washing machine and then putting the shower gel on the shelf in the bathroom. I left my slippers in the foyer and wore my sandals to step out. From the departmental store close by, I got Haldiram Boondi that comes with its own sachet of masala that you can put in the Raita for seasoning. For Dahi, I picked for two pouches of 'Amul Masti'.

When I came back home, I got the sweet whiff of Basmati rice and the spices that had gone in the Pulao. The missus had just opened the cooker and she was mixing the rice and the vegetables. It was really testing me: to have to wait any longer. I went to the kitchen and took out a bowl from the shelf. I poured a pouch of curd in it and beat it to a smooth consistency before emptying half the packet of Boondi and sprinkling an entire packet of masala in it. I mixed all of them with a large table spoon before leaving it in the bowl. While I was making the Raita, the missus had already kept the cooker on the dining table. It seemed that presently then, like me, instead of tearing into our food, she too was hiding her famishment with fortitude only because of culture imbued in us. But in her case, it was betrayed by her not emptying the Pulao in a serving bowl first. I quickly carried four plates and the bowl of Raita to the dining table. But we had to wait for a few more minutes because while my boy was ready soon, my girl took another ten minutes to come to lunch.

After the first few spoons of Pulao were eaten and the craving was abated, I asked "should we go out for dinner in the evening?" While my question was to the missus, the first to jump to answer was my boy who said "Mcdonald's", and immediately after him, my girl said "Chinese".

The missus nodded her head while at the same time, pulled out the spoon that had just dumped pulao in her mouth, and that was now descending to the cup of Raita in her plate. She slurped from the spoon and chewed delectably the squishy mix of pulao and raita in her mouth. I kept waiting expectantly. Finally, she swallowed and said "alright" in a matter-of-factly way. "You pick the place, but no burger and Chinese", she added next, and at the same time, gave a long stare to the children who swallowed their rising protest.

"We have tried most of the places I know. Today, we will go to whichever place you say". I said, trying to be nice.

"Bholenath". The missus uttered.

"What happened? Why are you calling out Lord Shiva?", I enquired anxiously.

"Not the lord, but Bhaiyya's cart", the missus answered.

"Where is that?"

"Oho, we keep passing by it whenever we go to D-Mart. You have seen it so many times, 'Bholenaath Chaat Bhandar'. He makes the best Paani-Puri around and his Chhole Tikia is awesome. I want to have one Pani-Puri and one Chhole Tikia for dinner.", the missus responded with finality in her tone.

"Really? I was asking about dinner, not some snacks.", I said, trying to be smart and mocking at the same time. "I thought you would choose some nice sit-in restaurant.", I said.

"If you don't want to listen to me, why do you ask then? You decide and I will come to wherever you say.", the missus said which

78   *Every Day is Another Day*

was smarter and more mocking than I had tried to be. She was now looking down and scraping her plate with her spoon. At this point, the children too jumped in saying "Papa, Bholenath will do. After that, we will go to Gupta Sandwich also."

I scooped some pulao from the cooker for her and said "Choole Tikia will be fine for me as well."

The missus looked happy and she let me serve her some more Pulao.

The evening played out as the missus had planned. The walk to Bholenath was a long one and so, we drove, but it was too crowded near it with no place to park close by. I had to drive further some two hundred meters to finally get a slot to push my car in. From there, we walked back to Bholenath.

After paani poori,chhole tikia, and dahi vada, as we were walking back, the missus said "DPji, maja aaya aaj. Let us eat ice-cream now. After eating spicy food, one should eat something cold".

"Really, who told you that?", I enquired pushing her by her shoulder, playfully

"I read that in a WhatsApp message", the missus said.

WhatsApp Woes

When enumerating indicators often, the most deserving and pertinent either get left out or get stacked below others that are less deserving and less pertinent. In thinking of aches, the head ache and the stomach ache come to the fore sooner than the ache of the heart. Sometimes, the heart ache may not find mention at all. If you come to think of it, tell me, is there an ache more distressing than the ache of the heart? Similarly, in thinking of deprivation, one is likely to think of the want of money, food, and perhaps even health, but never sleep. What an irony!

On that night too, I reached home only at about nine in the evening. By the time dinner was had, it was ten. After wiping my hands with a hand towel by the wash basin, I picked up my phone on which I saw a few office emails, I replied to some of them, not from the phone but from my laptop, which, once opened, doesn't shut down before at least an hour because I don't close it before that because the WIFI keeps working, the browser remains open, and there are Youtube, Netflix, Prime Video, and all.

After I closed my laptop, by which time the missus was already asleep, I tried to sleep but it took at least an hour for my mind to ease before I could actually sleep. And this way, I once again slept till late.

In the morning, I felt that I was shaking in my bed. I had no sense of it until I was vigorously shaking and jerking. Near my ribs, I felt a hand that was joggling me. I surfaced from deep sleep. I heard the sound getting louder. The shaking continued with someone yelling "stop it, stop it, get up, stop it". I groped with my right hand and after some fumbling, I finally found my mobile phone and I hit the stop button. I got up. Next to me, the missus was turning to her

Every Day is Another Day

side and now, her back was towards me. "Did we argue on something yesterday?" I thought. I stepped out of bed. "Good morning" I said. She acknowledged and smiled as she turned again lying straight and looking at me. "See if the children are up", she said. It was six in the morning. Six is also the time when the children get up to then get ready to catch their school bus by 7:15 AM.

This had been the way for more than a year having worked it out backwards from nine, when I have to be at my office. Get up at six, no matter what, and start the drive to office by quarter to eight.

First, I woke up the children. Then, rubbing the last vestiges of sleep off my eyes, I headed to the main door of our apartment to pick up the newspaper. It had been pushed from under the door with such force that it had skidded a couple of feet inside our living room. I find it at about the same place every day. l had to bend and pick it up. With my feet somewhat wide apart, I squatted a little and then, I bent no more than twenty degrees for my hand to reach the newspaper. I picked it up, not without a grunt though. I opened the door and stepped out. The milk bag was there the way it is put in its place every night, hanging by the door handle with the key hole peering from between its loop handles. Just that right then, the handles were taught as the bag was laden with two milk packets which the supplier had put in them like he puts them every morning by some time before six. 'When does he sleep?', I always think. Taking the milk bag, I closed the door before coming inside. Having put the milk packets on the kitchen platform, I opened the newspaper, sitting by the dining table. Some sounds were coming. They were pinching the inside of my ears and a tingling went through my teeth. The tea pan and the strainer were being pulled out from the mound of utensils washed and dumped, perhaps the last evening, in a plastic basket by the sink.

She was up.

Inside the kitchen, I could imagine what must be happening. One packet of milk would go inside the refrigerator and the other will be put to boil on the gas stove. The milk will be heated till it rises to just about the brim of the vessel, trying to peer down, and just before it keels over, the knob will be turned off. In the meantime, the tea decoction too will be ready. Almost every day, this chore, in which I play no part, gives me those ten minutes in which I soak in the headlines and the titbits.

She came with two cups of tea. Sitting across from me, she pushed one cup towards me. Straightaway, I picked it up and started sipping from it while going through the sports page to which, I had reached flipping through the newspaper. While I appeared to be reading, she asked 'what's the news today?'. "Not much and nothing more than what they were discussing on TV last night", I said.

I folded the newspaper before pushing it towards her. I got up from the dining table to go to our bedroom. I walked a bit faster, spurred by the tea and the biological urgency it induces in the morning. From the wall closet, I grabbed my towel and my underwear. My cell phone was still attached to the charger and lying on the table by the side of the bed. Detaching the charger from the phone's end, I carried the phone as well to the bathroom. The morning routine in the bathroom is a close to forty minutes affair and I always take my phone with me to manage and make good use of this time.

In designing it, from where would he have drawn his inspiration? Perhaps there were the constant rumblings in the stomach and the loosening of the bowels every time before the court of Her Majesty went into session and a well-judged response had to be pondered over well in advance to the anticipated questions. Therefore, it is likely that for the relief and musing to go hand in hand, Sir John Harington invented the English Flush Toilet towards the end of the sixteenth century. Sitting with the elbows on top of the knees and the chin resting on the palms, dumping the crap and picking the thoughts. Marvellous!

Having a modern version of this implement at my disposal, I sat and then unlocked my phone. The WhatsApp notification was there. At night, I had last checked my phone before I went to bed. "Who will message me during the night or so early in the morning?", I thought. I had some hint but I was still curious. I opened WhatsApp. There were five messages and all were in the family group. An uncle had sent a picture of a smiling infant with a 'Good Morning' caption. A couple of relatives had responded. This was their way of saying that rise early. 'Don't quack like a duck, soar like an eagle'. This message was from an uncle who retired from the Public Works Department as the Personal Assistant to the Chief Engineer. I saw the next message. This was a forward from a dear aunt who knows which tree's bark needs to be powdered and had for arthritis, which root's extract reduces blood sugar, how the lifelong abuse of one's body can be offset by having the juice of bottle gourd. This message though, was about the benefits of drinking a litre of water as soon as one wakes up: on empty stomach and before brushing one's teeth. The message's nature was preventive and not corrective unlike her usual messages. For alleviating any pain, you need to have the pain first. To reduce high blood sugar, you need to have diabetes first. The tone here was more prospective: do this one thing and there will be overall wellbeing in the times to come. The message was a bit long but interspersed here and there were words and phrases such as 'Ayurveda', 'Sages of India', 'our old tradition' which added to its appeal and credibility. The message had a positive effect on me. It was not asking anything difficult or that needed any prior preparation. It was a long message but the thing it was asking to do was to drink some more water than what generally people drink after getting up. After reading this message and then fiddling with the phone some more, I kept the phone in a niche in the bathroom that holds it and keeps it from getting wet. I went about my chores.

Having left the towel on the towel bar in the bathroom, I stepped out in my speedo underwear presenting the sight of a very well fed and indolent antithesis of Bikram Choudhary. I quickly put on my shirt and trouser, put some moisturiser on my face, and I was almost ready. Getting ready for office has been very expeditious for me since the time my palms have been dragging the moisturiser till the crown of my head and disciplining the few strands of inquisitive hair by pinning them to their place. I carried my belt and tie with me to the living room. I threw them on the sofa before sitting at the dining table. She was cutting an apple in neat wedges. On the dining table, on a bamboo trivet, there was a wok closed with its lid. Expectantly, I opened the lid and dejectedly, I put it back. In certain cases, doing the same thing every day is a mark of discipline, character, and such higher order traits that not only make you an exemplar to be emulated but also make you feel good about yourself. In certain other cases, the routine can blight the joys of life. While exercising everyday can lift your spirits, the same cannot be said about eating the same thing for breakfast every other day. "Poha again!", I uttered.

You don't want?

But yesterday also there was Poha.

She did not say anything. The children too were at the dining table drinking their Bournvita. "Did you see the message from Aunty?", I asked

Every Day is Another Day

"Which one?"

"The one that she sent today about drinking a litre water every morning on empty stomach. Let us try it from tomorrow."

"You do whatever you want. If you can continue with it for more than a week, I'll see." She challenged me.

As an afterthought, she enquired, by way of a remark: "So, you will not have tea in the morning from tomorrow?"

"I will have tea but after having the water", I said to assuage her doubt. I had hoped this would suffice but obviously, it did not. She looked up with some incredulity in her expression that was provoked by the missing 'when' in the sequence I established. Water and then tea. That is easy to understand. "But when?", that is what the furrowing of the brow had meant.

"But I'll have it later with breakfast", I clarified. You are not to eat or drink anything for about an hour after drinking water. You make the tea as usual. I'll have it later. "What have we bought the microwave for but for heating that which is to be had hot but which has gone cold", I said meaning it as a joke to which there was no reaction.

Having finished my breakfast, by which time, the children had finished their Bournvita, and the missus and the children had gone down to wait for the school bus, I picked my dish and spoon and dumped them in the sink. I scurried here and there to find my socks, my shoes, my watch. It took me a few moments to get ready and I was all set to leave for work. It was seven thirty already.

It was the next day and I got up at six again. Oftentimes, immediately preceding the commencement of anything new is anxiety or excitement or both. Since it is water that had to enter me and not the other way round, there wasn't any anxiety. Therefore, with only excitement, I readied myself to commence the routine of drinking a litre of water, first thing in the morning on empty stomach. After I shook my children out of their sleep, and made sure they did not fall back to sleep again by first switching off the air conditioner, and then the fan, then switching on the lights, and then pulling out their quilt, I put my mind again to the water business. Having picked up the newspaper and the milk packets, I went to the kitchen, filled my jug straight from the water filter before taking it and a tumbler to the dining table to drink all that water. When I was walking out of the kitchen, the missus was entering it, tying her hair behind her head. Once again, sounds came from the kitchen that pinched the inside of my ears.

Will you have tea?

Later.

She didn't answer.

I sipped the first glass slowly and took my time finishing it before filling up again. I could drink the second glass as well comfortably because my body needed the hydration. However, when I took the first sip of the third glass, I did not at all want to drink more. But then, taking it slowly and with short sips, I finished the third glass as well. The missus came to the dining table with her cup of tea. I was too engrossed in my task and she pulled the newspaper towards her.

How is it going?

This is too much to drink.

But beer, you and your friends drink like camels.

I filled the fourth and the last glass and gulped it down.

The rest of the morning was no different from the other days. For breakfast, I had my tea with a sandwich. I left my apartment at about seven thirty. The lift, the walk to my parking slot, driving out of my apartment complex and then coming onto the main road takes about ten minutes. My drive to office actually starts then. It usually takes me an hour and fifteen minutes to reach my office. I switched on the FM radio which makes it everything I need to settle in my drive. The radio jockey was playing a prank on someone. I waited for some song to start. It did, very soon. Listening to the FM, which was some songs interspersed in between a lot of drivelling from someone called an RJ who tries to be endearing but who instead, sounds very fatuous, I had driven for abcount 20 minutes and then, I was at the Vashi toll plaza. There were long queues of vehicles. After a few minutes, I was halfway inside the queue I had chosen. I was feeling the need to shift in my seat. I wriggled a bit. Things seemed fine. I settled again. There were now only two cars ahead of me at the toll booth. I pulled out my wallet from my right rear pocket to take out the change to pay. I looked up. I was now behind only one. The car ahead of me was taking longer than usual. I rolled down my window to peek out and check what was happening. I once again felt the unease. I wriggled in my seat again. The car ahead finally moved. I seemed to have taken a moment or so longer than what is acceptable to Mumbaikars to shift the gear and move. The restless one behind me honked as though it was only me in between him and salvation. Spurred by the honking, I lurched ahead to pay the toll after which, I manoeuvred my car to the right most lane. All of a sudden, my lower abdomen started to contract. There was a pressure building inside me. I started to feel it. The traffic was moving very slowly. It seemed like one of the lanes was being repaired. The pressure was not constant. It was radiating inside out, lessening, and then radiating again. I looked down, turned my head left and right and then I looked up again. The traffic was crawling. One part of my mind was saying 'screwed' and the other was saying 'It's OK. You can hold. It's only fifty more minutes to the office'. My car kept crawling along with the others. At the end of the Vashi flyover, there was a slight hold up, and the ensuing chaos. I swore at some of the drivers. To my relief, the traffic moved in about a couple of minutes and the road opened up again. I pressed the accelerator. The pressure radiated again. But this time, it did not ebb. It remained constant. I started to feel a vacuum between my legs. I panicked. I went to feel the vacuum that was beneath the seam of the crotch point of my trouser. By implication, I was assured that whatever is supposed to be there was actually there because even though it couldn't feel my hand, my hand could feel it. My mind screamed "O God!". My situation required my complete attention and any distraction could have had unspeakable consequences. I switched off the radio. I needed all my mind power to contract and restrain. Even though I was invoking my ch'i, things started to appear a bit blurred. My eyes dilated. I wanted to stop the car and run to the side of the road. I didn't care if they penalized me. But I was in the right most lane. There were four lanes of cars to my left and there was no place to stop. What could I do? There was an empty bottle of water tucked in the passenger side door. An idea crossed my mind. But peeing in a bottle while driving is impossible. I quickly abandoned the idea. I looked around to see if there was any place where I could stop and relieve myself. There was none. The stretch of road that I have to take to office, offers no chance of finding such a place. Mumbai can be cruel.

I wanted to let go. I was wearing Khaki coloured trousers. "Why not black?", I cursed myself. Time was passing by. Every second was seeming like ten. My breathing was shallow and I was panting.

Every Day is Another Day

I couldn't fill my lungs. That would then push my stomach. I was driving by pure reflex and muscle memory. I don't know how I reached that far but I was very close to the business district in which my office is. It was another just three kilometres of drive. At that point, my knees started to come together and my feet started to move apart. My back had straightened. My bladder was so full that I could feel it like a very taught inflated balloon that would burst any moment. I resolved 'just a little bit more'. Those last couple of kilometres, I drove like my car was a jet without wings. I could have taken off. I reached the parking in the basement of my office building and with a deftness hitherto unknown to even me, I put the car straight in the parking slot in one swift turn of the wheel. I opened the door to jump out. With the crescendo almost being reached in the final stage of the act, I missed a note. I forgot to take the seat belt off. I cursed myself. I took the seat belt off, grabbed my laptop bag and lunch box, and run towards the lifts. I had to reach the 6th floor. There were people around me waiting for the lifts to come. My face was flushed and my heart was pounding. The first lift arrived and I pushed my way inside it. A few people looked at me with scorn. I kept the 'I don't care' look. I pressed 6. There were other fingers that pressed 1 2 3 4 5 . Nooooooo! I cursed those who pressed 1 and 2. Why couldn't they just walk up a floor or two. WHY? I was standing inside the lift with my legs pressed tightly together, holding my bag and my lunch box in front of me – just in case. The sixth floor came. I was the only person to get out on that floor. I got out and ran. I flashed my tag at the door and it opened. I threw my bag and my lunch box in one of the chairs kept at the reception and I ran to the gents' room, pushing open the door with my momentum. There were three urinals. Two gentlemen were standing at either ends. I quickly took my place in the middle one, and in a speed faster than Schumacher, I pulled the zipper down and started relieving myself. I took a long breath and pushed. I lost my breath after some time and I couldn't push more. I inhaled and pushed again. There was considerable relief now that I felt. I look up and turned my head left and right. The two gentlemen had already left and there was no one in the rest room. By then, my breathing had become regular and I was experiencing a sense of relief that I had never experienced before. I could see perceptibly now. The light was seeming brighter than how it had seemed when I entered. I made sure that I didn't have to inhale and push again. It was all done. I zipped up and turned around. I saw myself in the mirror- a warrior who prevailed. I washed my hands and came out.

To my left, I saw the water dispenser. I just looked away and walked back to pick my stuff from where I had dumped them near the reception.

When I returned home in the evening, the children and the missus were watching TV. The children had had their dinner but the missus was waiting for me. By the time I washed up and changed, she had set the dinner on the dining table. As we started to eat, I sheepishly said "from tomorrow, I will have tea the way we normally have together." "Why, what happened?", she asked. As I started to recount the morning's event, though not very vividly, it was still enough to give the missus a choking fit as she laughed at my predicament while still having her food in her mouth.

Serial Entrepreneurs

A client meeting in Pune got confirmed on Wednesday. The meeting was on Friday. Considering that I had to travel from Mumbai, the client agreed to meet me at 2 PM. When I let the missus know that I would be traveling to Pune on Friday and be back by the same evening, she said "let us all go. It has been quite some time that we have not been to see Mummy and Papa".

But what about school?

"One day leave if they take, noting will happen. Anyway, they will cover the portion in tuition as well."

So, instead of the office cab, I decided to drive down to Pune with the missus and the children with the idea of noting down the exact to and from distance because the office reimburses the fuel expenses at Rupees twelve per kilometre.

We left home late in the morning at ten. From Kharghar in Navi Mumbai, my in-laws place at Baner in Pune is about two hours. We would have made the trip in time because the children had long lost their love for vada-paav at the food mall but they had found new love for burger and choco-lava cake at McDonalds. We had to stop in between for the children to eat while the missus and I had chai. We reached the in-laws place around 12:30. At 65, the mother-in-law was still very active but at 73, my father-in-law had suddenly started to look older and weaker as though the transition from the sixties into the seventies had sapped his verve.

When we entered the main gate, my father-in-law's old Honda Activa, which he refuses to sell or to just give away, was parked in front of his old Wagan-R that was covered in a plastic (or whatever they call its material) car cover. I could see that the air pressure in the tyres was less which meant that the car had not been driven for quite some time.

As soon as I parked my car outside the house, my mother-in-law came out because she was waiting in anticipation, peering through the window, after the missus called her on her cell phone as we were making a turn near Sadanand Hotel. By the time I switched off my car and was about to get down, the children had already jumped off from the rear and they were hugging their grandmother. When I got down, by which time the missus too got down, and walking around the front of the car, she was now to my left, my mother-in-law asked me 'kaise ho beta' in that sincere tone that is laced with love and regard in equal measure that is reserved only for sons-in-law. "Jee sab badhiya", I said before going near her and touching her feet. When we entered the house, my father-in-law came into the living room from somewhere inside the house. His crushed Kurta gave away that he was napping in his room. I touched his feet too before looking at my wrist watch, which was unnecessary because I had already seen the wall clock by which, it was already thirty minutes past twelve, and it was almost time for me to leave as I had to drive a long and tedious distance to Commerce Zone near Yerwada. After I kept the bags in a corner in the living room, when I said that I would be leaving for my meeting, my mother-in-law just wouldn't have anything of what I had to say and insisted that I had my lunch which was already ready but for the rotis which she wanted to make fresh. And so, I quickly ate a couple of rotis, some rice, aaloo bhindi subzee, moong dal, and finally, one aamba barfi from Chitale Bandhu which, my father-in-law would have bought that very morning. It was nearly one in the afternoon when I could finally leave. When the missus asked when I would be back, I said that I will be late, that I will be returning around ten thirty or eleven in the night, that I had to meet Himanshu, who the missus knew as my friend from school, and since the in-laws were also around while I was mentioning this, they too knew that I wouldn't be having dinner at home.

I reached Commerce Zone just in time for my meeting. The meeting got over by 3:30 PM. Not having much to do thereafter, I came to Hinjewadi Phase II to our company's sprawling development center there by 5 PM so as to do some pending work which was nothing beyond a few emails and a couple of phone calls. By the time all this was done, it was already 6:30 PM. I had already let Himanshu know that I would be at Hinjewadi by sending him a message on WhatsApp which he acknowledged with a thumbs up.

I was waiting for my phone to ring any time. The plan was arranged between Himanshu and me on phone calls on Wednesday, re-confirmed on Thursday and then, confirmed again on WhatsApp while I was driving back from Commerce Zone . ' BTW all is going well. Will call before starting. YAM. OK. NNTR'.

Each confirmation fortified more the original commitment. You see, for corporate slaves, commitments to friends and family are the most brittle and one doesn't even flinch a bit before breaking one because one is as often the disappointed as often one is the breaker, averaging things out. It could be a last-minute phone call or a meeting quickly convened that can spoil any personal plan. We had already discussed half past six as the time around which we would leave our offices. Sure enough, the phone rang, just about in time. Himanshu asked, "ready to leave?" I said yes, relieved that the plan had stayed.

Himanshu had to start from Phase 1 and I had to start from Phase 2 of Hinjewadi IT Park.

Our destination was Saundarya Garden: Family restaurant and Bar that is made to look cool by its temporary structure mostly on wooden poles and tarpaulin that successfully caught the fancy of wannabes. It has a separate family section in the rear. I have always wondered which families come here. The front section though is the place for the ubiquitous IT engineers to drink and eat.

Himnahsu had to drive 3.5 Kms and I had to drive 4.5 Kms to reach our destination by 7 PM. I reached the Hinjewadi circle to find myself at the rear end of the traffic block with a Mahindra Bolero squeezing on my left, its side mirror almost touching mine and just short of scuffing it. I turned my head to confront the idiot to find a stern looking face already staring at me, scratching his beard and mumbling something, directed at me in the patois of which it was clear that he was abusing me but the exact abuses weren't to my comprehension. I looked straight. The signal turned green, and the traffic started to move. Some space emerged between the car ahead of me and mine. I did not move. The one behind me honked. I let the blighter and his Bolero pass and then I moved, pushed by the din of honking coming from behind.

I continued straight towards the Hinjewadi-Wakad flyover that goes over the Mumbai-Bangalore highway connecting the infotech park where people work to the city where people live like the hourglass where the sand is in either end but not in both unless it is on its journey from one side to the other through the narrow neck. The flyover was about two kilometers from the signal where I was. I kept crawling along the road in the heavy traffic. In a few minutes, about two hundred meters before the flyover, I saw the neon sign of Saundrya Garden. I was already in the left lane to easily get off the road. It was ten minutes past seven as I noticed the time in the digital clock of my car. The parking attendant, who was also the security guard, directed me to a large empty plot abutting Saundarya Garden where only a few cars were parked at that time. I had already noticed Himanshu's car in the parking and I put my car next to his. I got down and called him on his cell phone - "Himanshu, I am here. Where are you?"

"Come inside, I just reached and found a table for us."

I locked my car having tucked my laptop bag behind the driver seat. I walked to cross over to the other side to the main entrance through a gap in the hedge. I noticed a sign proclaiming 'Parking at owner's risk'. I turned back to collect the laptop bag. Himanshu was sitting at a table that was second to the left of the service manager's deck. We are friends of the vintage and kind who don't need to hug every time we meet. I grabbed my chair that was a metal frame with padding for the seat and the back. "What should we have?", I asked. "The same thing", Himanshu answered. It was a nip of Old Monk rum for me and a bottle of Tuborg beer for Himanshu that is tres chic and so are some craft beers leaving Kingfisher to the uber loyal. Old Monk is a cue for taste and not for cheap preference. Instead of ordering affordable whiskey, I prefer to order Old Monk. No judgements there. After the drinks arrived, Himanshu swigged half a mug straight while I took a sip of Rum mixed with cold water from a bottle of Bisleri. Tossing some peanuts in his palm, that are served complimentary with the drinks, Himanshu asked "what's happening these days?"

My usual answer to this usual question was interrupted by the waiter who came just then to enquire if we were ready to order something to snack on with our drinks. He handed us each a menu card that we quickly kept aside. First, we didn't need to order anything fancy and secondly, Saundarya Garden doesn't offer anything fancy. Himanshu went for half a portion of tandoori chicken and asked the waiter to get 'any' paneer kebab for me with a mixture of apathy and disdain that meat eaters have for vegetarians. The waiter left taking both the menu cards with him.

As it would betide, the break in conversation allowed me to segue into something more significant than knowing each other's wellbeing and whereabout.

"Himanshu, that paneer kebab, at least two hundred rupees he will charge us for that", I said.

"Ya, that much is the minimum these days unless it is a street side shack"

"Even if he uses Amul paneer, the 200 grams packet comes for seventy. These guys must be ordering in bulk from a local dairy and it should cost them much less. Let us say it costs him fifty and he uses all the 200 grams for my kebab, how much will it really cost to make the whole dish? With the spices and condiments, the fuel and labour, etc. it should not cost more than 100. The profit margin is at least 100%", I went on.

Himanshu drowned the rest of his beer which was almost half the mug in one gulp. The waiter rushed to refill his mug from the already half-consumed bottle that was left on our table with the loose bottle cap covering its mouth after the first mug was served. "Sir, repeat?", he asked only Himanshu as I had just about made my second drink. He left on getting the confirmation.

Not only picking the thread from where I left but also dragging it along, Himanshu said "this restaurant business is an amazing one, once it starts running well. But there is great headache as well of managing the kitchen, the chef and the cooks, the staff. Then there are the government agencies for tax, hygiene and all that".

Now, if you are just about to take a bite off a slice of a well topped pizza, and at that very moment, a hearsay or internet relying diet enthusiast who follows the latest dietary fad that happens to be Keto these days, appears all of a sudden and says "O my God, so many carbs", how would you feel? I felt the same way on hearing Himanshu.

"But Himanshu, there is headache in everything", I carried on, trying to be wise.

"But there is investment also", he quickly added.

I leaned forward a bit with both my hands on the table and ran a quick survey to make sure that none of the service staff was too close to overhear us.

"Himanshu, of this place, the land must be theirs only. For restaurant, the structure is a temporary one calling itself 'open air'. That is smart. The food is a just bit above average. What I mean to say is that so long as the taste of food is better than what is served in office canteens, you can get away with it. Anyway, who really knows these days what is good food? Just make sure your stuff is not bad. People need to eat out, and they need places so that if the best place is full, the next best can be tried and then the next one till you really can't lower your standard any more. Quantity bro – democratization of food. Like software as a service, food as a service – FaaS (laughs happened at this point as the wit was not lost on either of us). Luck has favoured this place in putting it where it is on this main road from where it is so easily visible and accessible. These are the kinds of things that would require some planning. Otherwise, just look at the profits they make even on the humble paneer tikka. Boss, I am telling you, we should seriously think of starting something to do with food."

I finished the gab by emptying my drink and putting the glass on the table with a mild thud to make the last point. In the same momentum, I poured the last of the remaining rum in my glass which was something in between a small peg and a large peg which explains why the last peg was a bit mild.

Taking a sip from the new peg, I was eager to continue the conversation as I took Himanshu's lack of interjections as his keen attention to all that I was saying.

"With Swiggy and Zomato and their likes, we just need to be on their platform for food pick-up. There won't actually be any need for a large place, sit-down setup and all that", Himanshu added. I was right about his keen attention.

"Boss, at an average order size of even two hundred, should it be difficult to scale to just two hundred orders a day? That is forty thousand per day which is twelve lakhs in a month which is one crore forty-four lakhs in a year. At, at least hundred percent profit margin, that is seventy lakhs in profit", Himanshu said with excitement that he was unable to contain.

Sipping that last of the rum that was left in my glass, I bitterly lamented to Himanshu how we waste time by not doing anything. Noticing that my drink was finished, Himanshu called for the waiter and asked me at the same time, 'repeat?'.

Repeat here means repeat of the last order for me which was a nip of rum. I said, "Boss, I need to drive home".

"Are yaar, capacity kam ho gayi tumhari!", taunted Himanshu which was a more effective way of having his way without actually insisting. Instead of another nip, I settled for a 90 ml peg with the endorsement of Himanshu, and asked for a bottle of Coke as well this time, to mix it with. Himanshu asked for another beer. While we were waiting for our drinks to arrive, Himanshu leaned back in his chair pensively smoking his Gold Flake Kings. Still looking up, he enquired about the capital required with the confidence of not only someone wanting to start a business but also of someone having the money to invest.

"Boss, even if we take everything on the higher side, it should not be more than twenty lakhs in the first year including rent, all capital expenditure and wages. Only take away. So, the cost of furniture, décor, waiting staff: just not there", I said having figured it out in my mind on the fly and doing some quick computations on the tissue paper.

The conversation was going forward intensely with Himanshu asking difficult questions like they do in Shark Tank and blowing holes in the story. "What about repeat business? In the food business, you need regular customers. That takes time to build. Then, will not people want change of taste? Why should they stick to us?", he asked all these questions all at once.

Egged on by the enthusiasm I was feeling and the intensity of the conversation which you will most likely mistake as an alcohol induced prattle, I said " Himanshu, the world that we are in today, loyalty is to the platforms like Swiggy and Zomato and not to the place. Within the platform, people want choice. We add to that. Look around. This city is full of single people who need to order food daily. Every year, hordes of new IT engineers come. So, you are new to them. Then, look at the so many management and engineering colleges around. Every year, new batches come. You have numbers.

Who needs loyalty?"

As it happens sometimes, an idea erupts impromptu in the course of speaking. "Boss, we can differentiate in the market. Normal food is one thing and then there is all this Chinese and Italian and Mexican and such stuff. But traditional Indian food, people still want to eat but don't know how to make on their own and no place serves it. Take for example Kathal ki Sabzee. That is a niche", I said.

"Bhai, this is sounding very good. That last thing you said about kathal ki sabzee, that has potential. We need to sit very soon and make a business plan. For how long will we keep doing the same business analysis, coding and all that?", Himanshu said.

As I was finishing my last drink, I noticed that Himanshu's mug was also empty. When we were just about to once again start being spiteful of our jobs, Himanshu looked at his watch and let me know that it was already ninety thirty and we ought to be leaving. He raised his hand and wrote something in the air which was picked up by the captain of the waiting staff who was standing next to the service deck as the sign to get the bill. Himanshu paid the bill when it came. Between close friends, the question of going dutch just does not arise.

We walked out of Saudarya Garden towards Anna's paan shop that is at its periphery but within the boundary which means that this is another revenue source for Saundarya Garden that I had ignored until that day but of which I made a mental note then. Having a paan at Anna's shop before leaving is more of a ritual than a requirement. When we reached it, there already were a few people there who were a mix of men asking for their Classic Mild or Classic Regular or Gold Flake Kings or the sissies who smoked more under peer pressure asking for their menthols or oranges or such flavours that I don't even feel like speaking of. Himanshu asked for a packet of 10 of

Gold Flake Kings and a meetha paan. I asked for a saada masala. The meetha paan was ready made that Anna's apprentice took out from the small refrigerator and gave it to Himanshu who started munching it. Anna then started to make my saada masala.

"Hey, last time we spoke about floriculture and you were to find out from some friend of yours from Satara about leasing some land close to the Bangalore highway. What happened to that?", Himanshu reminded me.

"Arre yaar, I just forgot about that. But I am going to do that over the weekend and let us speak again", I assured him.

Anna gave me my paan that I put in my mouth. My fingers were stained red with the juice of the paan that I wiped using a couple of tissue papers Anna gave me on demand because while everyone's fingers get stained during the paan's journey from the hand to the mouth, not everyone asks for tissue paper. Some rub their palms together or, lick their fingers or, just wipe them on their jeans to notice it in the morning when sober. I dumped the tissue papers in the waste bin before paying for the paans and the cigarette packet. We chewed on the paan for some time until Himanshu simultaneously yet quickly took some drags of a cigarette from the fresh packet we just took and stubbed it when nearly half of the stick still remained. That was a lot of money just crushed under the boot. At the parking lot, the security guard cum parking attendant, when he saw us, started to walk in our direction. Some change of cash, that Anna had returned, was in my shirt's pocket. I give the man fifty rupees. I eased his discomfiture on not knowing which patron to attend to when two of them come at the same time by opening the door of my car myself so that he could open the door of Himanshu's car for him. I was the first to reverse. I honked my good bye that Himanshu acknowledged by sticking his hand out of the window and waving. We parted ways and went home.

We keep meeting whenever the chance comes to hem and haw and have a few good drinks, make our new entrepreneurial plans that never move beyond our discussion because of uncle Newton's cardinal principle.

An object will remain at rest or move at a constant speed in a straight line unless it is acted on by an unbalanced force. When his mind pushed out this cardinal principle followed quickly by two more creating the famous triplet, that is, his three famous laws, Sir Issac Newton became the father of modern Physics. But in becoming that, he also became, if not the father, then the uncle of Metaphysics. It requires a great amount of force to stop an enterprising man from doing what he believes in, or to make an unimaginative one do anything other than staying on the well beaten path. But unlike the enterprising man where the force to stop him comes from outside fuelled by one or more of envy or competition or small mindedness, or the rule book, the force to move the unimaginative has to come from within. This is why, perhaps it is far easier to stop someone compared to arousing one. The hand of the system comes easily but hard on those few, to stop them, who clamour for everyone's rights while the majority keep enduring all the difficulties silently. All despots know this and this is how they maintain their hold: by the inertia of the silent who do not get aroused. If you know anything about the Chennai Test match where India lost to Pakistan, it was easy for Pakistan to finally get Sachin Tendulkar out and win it because the rest of the team just did not make any runs: one was unstoppable and the rest did not move because of the same thing - Inertia. As can be seen, Uncle Newton's cardinal principle is applicable generally. However, in the case of me and my friend Himanshu, it is applicable in particular. We have so many plans and that is all.

Every Day is Another Day

Information Overload

After meeting Himanshu, I reached my in-laws' place in about 15 minutes. Since the porch was the permanent abode of my father-in-law's car, I parked my car parallel to the boundary wall. As I crossed the short flight of stairs onto the veranda, the missus opened the door, perhaps because of the clank of the iron gate that I opened, which caught her attention. While I had my mouth shut tight, she still sensed it.

"Are you drunk?"

"mmm"

"What if mummy and papa come to know?"

On entering the living room, I sensed that the missus was alone downstairs. "Is everybody asleep?", I asked. "Yes, mummy and papa are sleeping. The children too got very tired and they are in their room", the missus said. I did not say anything more and climbed upstairs to our room on the first floor, carrying my laptop bag with me. I changed into my shorts and t-shirt and stretched on the bed. I was staring at the ceiling when the missus came with two bowls of vanilla ice-cream. "Papa got this in the evening", she said before handing one bowl to me.

We spent the next two days mostly at home but for the evening on Saturday when we first went to the Chatushringi temple and then drove down to Dhole Patil road to have parathas at Nandu's. We returned to Mumbai on Sunday at around 6:30 PM having started from Baner at 4 PM. As soon as we reached home, I quickly changed into some loose clothes and stretched on the bed. In the more than two hours of driving, my stomach was tightly compressed in between my chest and my jeans' waist band. Whenever I looked down, the bulge out would appear right below the sternum and arc out before arching in from below the waist. The buttons down from the fourth one were taut against the button holes, and the gaps between them were like gaping mouths through which my while vest was visible. All the while, there was a good amount of discomfort because of which, I would keep shifting turning in my seat. With about half an hour of lying still in my bed, I felt better.

Things were all well for the next few months until trouble visited me again, and in this visit, it told me that knowledge has to be first paid for through labour, humility and patience and then one has to wait and hope for it to visit the seeker. And, when it comes, if at all, instead of settling the inquisitive, it makes his desire insatiate. True knowledge opens a window peering through which, what all one knows is dwarfed by the magnitude of all that is there to know. That is humbling. But to us netizens, we have the tools to look-up in a trice, anything we want to know. That is enabling, yet that which comes so simply and to so many is not knowledge but information that fills the ego with so much air that instead of bowing to the vastness of the still to be known, the dork feels he is omniscient. Very rightly, the infrastructure feeding this is called not the knowledge highway but the information highway.

The information highway has many twists and bends that could be fatal to anyone speeding on it but unlike any real highway, there are no warning signs here. Getting off it as soon as one can seems to be the only way to wellbeing and sanity, and to that, credence and confirmation came through the experience of shit happening. I recall that incident, vividly.

For some days, a nagging pain in my back had been troubling me. I was believing that the pain shall soon pass, and pass on its own. After all, who rushes to the doctor on the first day of fever, or as soon as the head ache or the stomach ache starts, or the day the nose is choked and the body is jolted by the vigour of the sneeze? But on that day which was a Saturday, the lack of other urgencies like getting to office, or sending the proposal, or finishing the presentation come what may, made the pain in my back get a large share of my attention. That made me feel it more than what I felt on the few days that had already gone by. I was in the bedroom lying on the bed as anyone complaining of any pain would be.

The missus walked inside the bedroom with a hot water bottle that looked dull, in brick red colour. Handing it over to me, she said "use this, you will feel better." She sat close to me on the bed, near the edge. I turned on my side, in the direction away from her, so that she could help with the fomentation. Her nearness is always assuring; the gentleness and empathy only the feminine can bestow. She kept moving the hot water bottle around my lower back, never keeping it pressed to the same spot for long. After a few minutes, she broke the silence by saying "Sunil will be back home by seven in the evening. I will call Anita to ask him to come and see you. I have been asking you to go and see a doctor for the whole week. But when do you listen to anyone?" She emphasized the accusation in the end.

Now, Sunil is the Doctor who lives on the 12th floor in our building. Anita, his wife and the missus first started to interact, and this eventually led to our families getting to know each other.

"I will see a doctor. Keep Sunil out of this. I will go and see a specialist at Apollo hospital in the evening. I will need to call them and fix an appointment", I said.

Specialist! she exclaimed. "Why do you need to see a specialist for back pain?", she asked.

Before I could say anything, she added "Sunil will see you and then he will suggest if something more has to be done."

"Arre baba, Sunil is a general physician", I said.

"He is an M.D. He will know", she said with an indication of finality and imposition. Leaving the hot water bottle near me, she just got up and stomped out of the bed room, her irritation getting the better of her.

Letting go at this point, I pinned the hot water bottle to my back holding it with my left hand and then turned to lie supine in my lungi and sando vest (While girlfriends despise the lungi and the vest as belonging to the proletariat, the wives, unadmitted by them, do not mind their husbands covered in such a simple way not because the lungi and the vest together offer any sartorial elegance but because they make the man of the house unappealing to any other woman). I kept lying in bed staring at the ceiling. This pain had started a little over a week back. There was some unease already that I could feel but it was on the Friday of the preceding week that I really felt it late in the afternoon in my office. It wasn't a debilitating pain but a nagging one. I endured the drive back home that day, constantly shifting in my seat. One look at my face and the missus did not miss that something was not right with me. She enquired and I let her know of the pain. What then followed were some over the counter pain killers from the pharmacy close by and the advice of and adherence to rest over that weekend. On Monday morning, the pain was still there though I should say I had slept well during the night. That was when she asked me to see a doctor which I did not.

She once again came in the bedroom. This time, she was carrying the dried clothes she had taken down from the clothesline in the balcony. She had to now fold them neatly and then stack them in the wall closet. She smiled at me and asked "how are you feeling now?" I nodded, signaling that all was well with me.

"Should I rub some Moov on your back?", she asked. I waved my hand to say no by way of gesticulating. The hot water bottle did seem to have given me some momentary relief.

The missus was busy with her stuff and the children in theirs leaving me alone in the bedroom where, confined to my bed, I had nothing much to do. But, for how long can one be in a do-nothing state unless one is hibernating? If there is a scab, there is also the irresistible urge to scratch it. I exhaled completely and pulled my abdomen inside, my navel almost touching my spine. This pulled the muscles in my back and I let it go at the very moment beyond which there would have been a cramp. I gasped and my belly quickly retrieved and concomitantly, took back its convex shape. I was trying to locate the exact point of my pain but to no avail.

I opened my laptop to while away the time. The usefulness of Netflix and Amazon Prime Video can be realized only by perpetual indolence, or an induced period of sloth that I was a victim of. Since I was not already a few episodes into a web series to simply carry on from where I had stopped last, there was a slight struggle initially in deciding what to watch because of the wide choice available. I finally settled for some movie, the name of which I can't recall now, that a friend had recommended very strongly and the online reviews indicated that not watching it would be like missing something in life. The sounds were carried to my ears by the head phones obscuring all the other sounds so that I was neither disturbing nor getting disturbed.

It's was a nearly three hours movie. About an hour into it, the missus came to the room. As I looked at her, she first sighed and then swiftly came to the far side of the bed where my head was popped on a couple of pillows. The laptop was perched on my chest. She showed some spiral kind of flexibility by turning her neck, twisting her body at the waist and bending a bit, all at the same time to first have a closer look at what I was watching and then, to yank off my head phone. Before I could hit pause, she said "I have called you ten times for lunch so loudly, the whole building would have heard. Only you are not able to hear me".

Since the head phone was still attached to the laptop, without saying anything, I took it from her and together with the laptop, put them aside on the bed. I got up slowly and mindfully, and walked to the dining table. She was already at the table putting the Chhole in steel bowls and placing them in the plates kept ready for us. There was the usual chitter chatter but it was mostly between the missus and the children. I was eating in silence. My daughter did ask in between "what happened to papa?" because I was too silent, to which the missus said "papa has back ache", to which, my daughter just interjected with 'mm' and not even 'hmm' because her mouth was full with a big piece of poori.

After the lunch, the missus carried my plate and bowl to the

Every Day is Another Day

sink not letting me do so as I was technically unwell and getting the sympathy that naturally followed.

After the lunch, I was once again back in my bed: sprawled. When lunch is Puri and Chhole, it is seldom had in moderation to keep the meal light. And, if the heavy meal happens to be lunch, it takes a unique soporific characteristic that is stronger than any other urgency or temptation relegating them to irrelevance compared to the impending sleep. I dozed off. I slept for around two hours from 2 PM to 4 PM. After I got up, I once again opened my laptop. Netflix was still open on the browser. An inquisitive streak rose in me and I opened a new tab on the browser, and in the google search box, I typed "causes and remedies for back pain". The search result was a long one, and I read a few from the listing. After that, I had to fight some terrible emotions before I could hit on play again on the still paused movie.

In the evening, at about a little past seven, the doorbell rang. The missus opened the door to find Sunil, still formally dressed and adjusting his eye glasses. "Aaiye Bhaisaab (Please come, brother)", she said earnestly. Sunil tried to take off his shoes before entering.

"Are, rehne deejiye bhiasaab. Aise hee aa jaaiye. (Oh!, let it be brother. Come in without any hassle)", the missus said.

I observed this from the straight back chair in which I was seated. I had changed into a cotton lower and a round neck T-Shirt discarding my lungi and vest a few minutes prior to Sunil's coming in deference to the minimum rules of the etiquette of receiving someone in your home. I tried to get up when Sunil entered, but he gestured me to remain where I was.

"What happened to you, my friend?", he asked straightaway as though he had already decided this to be the first thing to say on entering our house.

"Severe back pain", the missus jumped in before me and took control of the situation.

"OK. Let me see. Why don't you lie down on the diwan?", Sunil said

I followed more than the brief. Since it was my back pain that needed examination, I went prone on the diwan. Sunil rolled and pushed my T-Shirt upwards and felt my lower back with his fingers.

"For how long this pain has been there?", he asked.

"For more than a week now", I said.

He asked me to get back up and sit. "Looks like a muscle pull. Did you do anything unusual or lift something heavy?", he asked.

"No, nothing that can be called unusual", I said after getting up, and while pulling down and adjusting my t-shirt.

She interjected again saying "arre Bhaisaab, you know these children of our community who play cricket in our common area, just some days back, he barged into these small boys, snatched their bat and made them bowl to him for half an hour. Is that not unusual to start swinging the bat all of a sudden? And then, the next day, there was some problem with the water heater in the bathroom attached to our bedroom. So, he carried a large bucket of hot water from the common bathroom to the one inside. From the evening of that day, he is uneasy with back pain. One day he swings and the other day he lifts a full bucket. And see, he is not admitting to anything."

"How is this unusual or heavy? If I was bowling for half an hour, that would have been unusual. And, carrying a bucket of water is a normal thing that people do at home. "What do you say Sunil?", I asked for reassurance.

"It's nothing much. It's a spasm in the lower back. I am prescribing a muscle relaxant, some pain killer, a gel to apply. If you feel acidity, I am writing an antacid as well. Take it. If possible, take off on Monday and rest. You should be fine in a day or two", Sunil said.

True to what I was suspecting, Sunil didn't go beyond the tick in the box kind of questions such as 'for how long you have been having the problem?', 'how much is the problem?', 'what did you do to get the problem?', and then prescribe some pills and rest. This is why I needed to see a specialist. With her being around, I was not getting the opening I wanted. While Sunil was busy scribbling the prescription on a piece of paper that I had to tear for him from my note book, the doorbell rang. The boy from the grocery shop outside our apartment complex had come to deliver a few things the missus had ordered on telephone. She was now busy settling the transaction.

Using the chance that had presented itself, I asked, "Sunil, should I get an MRI or PET scan done?"

"Do you mean X-Ray?", he asked.

"No, MRI of the abdomen", I reiterated.

Perhaps sensing that I was dithering and not coming to the point, Sunil looked at me suspiciously before asking "is there any other problem you have?".

You see, there is this constant bloating in my stomach. At times, there is a radiating pain also. I have been taking ENO for some days already, at times, twice or thrice in a week.

That is acidity you have.

That is what I too thought before this back pain also started.

By this time when we were holding off each other, the missus had seen the grocery boy off and turned towards us. She seemed to have overheard the last bit of our conversation.

Bhiasaab, he has chronic problem of gas. What do you call it? Yes 'Flatulence'. First, he has no control on his eating. He will eat anything at any time. And today, for 4 pooris, he ate 4 bowls of chhole. Look at the size of his stomach. Sunil turned his head towards me and actually started to stare where the missus wanted him to look.

"You know, a big stomach can also sometimes give you back pain. Why don't you do something to actually lose some girth?", he said. A sermon on fitness was the last thing on my mind. "If an athlete is fit, so is a Sumo wrestler", I wanted to say but I did not because in making my point, I would have had to admit that I was closer to a Sumo than to an athlete in how I looked. I was irked because here I was discussing something serious and these two were looking at the fragments and not at the larger picture. The time had come for me to come straight and not obliquely. "Sunil, what I was thinking was that back pain and heaviness in the stomach, if happening at different times, could be seen as different problems. But, if they occur simultaneously, perhaps they may be related?", I said.

But they can happen simultaneously if you eat like the way Bhabhi explained and you suddenly exert your body by doing the kind of things you did.

But Sunil, if they are together, it may suggest some other problem also. Should we not investigate?

Arre, there is no problem. I am telling you; your back pain will subside soon.

But what about say some tumor inside?

Oh! No, no. There is nothing like that.

A lump inside the stomach can cause back pain, and a feeling of heaviness may accompany it.

You are unnecessarily worrying. There is nothing wrong like that with you.

I searched on Google. It was explained in so much detail.

Sunil had been very patient all this while. In his mild-mannered way, he kept on assuring me that there was nothing amiss with me other than the spasm. On my furthering my line of argument with him, Sunil chuckled mildly, but this time, there was some derision in that. Even though she was silently listening to us, I don't know why, but the missus was looking conscious and embarrassed.

I was not in the mind to give up easily, but before I could open my mouth, the missus, with that tone of finality she often uses, said "arre, Bhaisaab spent five years doing MBBS, then another two years on his specialization and then, his so many years of practice. Will google foogle know more than Bhaisaab?

What could I have said to that? The matter came to rest. Sunil started to get up to leave but the missus asked him to wait. She ran inside the kitchen and quickly came back holding a tray with two glasses of water, some savoury dish in one small bowl, and a couple of barfis in the other. She held the tray first in front of Sunil and he picked up a glass of water. The missus then kept the tray on the center table and handled the other glass to me. Despite his protestations, Sunil couldn't leave before having some of the savoury and an entire burfi.

Anyway, by Monday, I was all fine with the pills and gel Sunil had prescribed for me. I did not have to take leave on Monday, and I was quite gay and relaxed because after a few stressful days with all kinds of thoughts in my mind, I was relieved that I did not have a tumour in my abdomen. But the missus was not at all amused. Sunil did not adhere to professional ethics where he had to maintain patient confidentiality. He told Anita, Anita told Surabhi and Mrs .Saxena, and like a wildfire spreads, almost the entire ladies gang knew, and they did not miss the chance to have a go at the missus when she enquired about something while walking with her group and one of them said " ask Jha ji to google na", and all of them guffawed. How mean!

Walking on the treadmill

There are two guys who have, of late, made my life hell. Both are old, older than me, but they still make the missus swoon. One is an ex-fashion model Milind Soman who is now a fitness freak, and the other is Salman Khan. So long as the missus was in love with their faces, things were fine because such love can be called a fan's admiration about which any husband can be fine without feeling cuckolded. However, when the missus fell in love with their bodies, this took a very different meaning. The missus, obdurate that she is at times, let me know of these loves of her when out of nowhere, she said "see, how some men maintain themselves as they grow old. Look at Milind Soman and Salman, and look at you. Why don't you also exercise and become fit?" She said this leaning against the pillows in the bed while I had just changed into my shorts and sleeveless vest for the night. Now, the moment of this quip, if it can be called that, was significant because in shorts and vest, I should be evoking passion in the missus but it seemed, I had evoked some disgust, and before I just collapsed under this affront to my self-esteem, the missus added "how fit and handsome you were when we married", on hearing which, I got some succour. "But yaar, these guys are compelled to maintain good bodies because of their profession, for guys like me, where is the time?", I said. The missus was still looking at her phone, and not looking at me, and then she said "faltu baaten mat karo. Every morning, I can see from our balcony, some men of your age run for at least half an hour. Just see how fit and fine they are for their age, and how good they look". This was too much for me because now, the missus brought the competition too close.

The very next day, I got up at 5:30, and while the missus was still sleeping. Using the torch light of my mobile phone, after very gingerly opening the wardrobe, I pulled out my shorts and t-shirt, and by 6:00, I was ready to step out. When I was tying my shoe laces, the missus came to the living room, having just woken up. "Where are you going?", she asked. I looked up and said "you only were saying last night that I should start exercising, and so, I am starting from today." Since generally, missuses are matter-of-factly, she just said "Okay, pull the door when you leave and close it properly, I am going to the bathroom." This way, my exercising routine started.

In about a month, I progressed from walking four rounds of our walkway to walking about seven which would take me about half an hour. But even after a month, I could see no effect of this on my body. One day, out of frustration, I decided that it was time for me to start jogging like the fit men who would get ahead of me twice around the walkway when I wouldn't even have finished one full round of it. And so, I did run but in going not even hundred meters, I felt a deep burning in my chest that started to heave, I felt my heart pounding, my mouth opened wide as I couldn't suck in enough air, my legs refused to lift up and move, and I stopped. Just at that moment, the joggers overtook me again, and while they were turning the corner which was a little ahead, one of them turned his head, looked at me, and smiled, which felt like a mocking smile. I continued my walk and as I came near the club house, I thought of walking inside and going to the gym because that day, my mind was not in walking because of which I had tried jogging in which I had failed miserably, but still on the path of doing something other than walking, I entered the gym. Opening its glass door slowly, instead of walking in confidently, first, I pushed my head through the half

Every Day is Another Day

open door, and then my body followed, there were some young men and college going boys, some were pumping iron, and some were walking around with a swagger, but all of them gave me just one look, and went back to doing whatever they were doing. Like in every new place, I was feeling tentative and out of place, I was wearing a fake smile, just looking around here and there without knowing what to do, and just then, from somewhere, clad in a black lower and a black t-shirt, someone walked up to me and said "yes sir, I am in the instructor here. What would you like to do?", and I felt relieved. I said "I have never been to a gym before, I need to start exercising and lose some weight", in a very candid way. "Okay sir, since we are just starting, you do fifteen minutes of walk on the treadmill and then do fifteen minutes on the elliptical", the trainer said, to which, when I gave him a confused look, he pointed to a machine on which there were pedals to stand on and two long poles jutting out vertically. "But I just finished my walk, should we then start with this machine?", I asked. "Okay sir", the instructor said which I liked then but which was actually his way of not pushing and wasting his time with the lazybones, which, on my own, I learnt later. The instructor's name is Eijaz, who has a flat stomach, big arms, and a massive chest. Meeting Eijaz on that day gave me a lot of confidence that something good will definitely happen to my body if I stick around with him.

After my first day at the Gym, I felt so nice that I completely abandoned the idea of walking outside around the walkway, and I started going to the gym every morning. After the first two days, Eijaz tried making me do some exercises calling them by funny names like squats, sit-ups, mountain climbers, lunges but he gave up quickly because I would not do any of these because I just could not, especially the one where I nearly burped out after the second of another funnily named exercise called Burpee of which Eijaz wanted me to do ten. I continued with my humble walk.

I had well settled in this routine, so much that it was now the fourth month of my regularly going to the gym to walk on the treadmill. After this long adherence, the positive effects of this walking routine were being felt by me but to others, such subtle changes were not visible.

I got up once again on time for my walk. After having some water in the kitchen, I went back to our bedroom to take out my gym wear from the hangar nailed to the inside of the door. Whatever combination of gym garments I decide on for the next day, I put them here at night for quick and hassle-free reclamation in the morning. For that day, it was a Grey T-Shirt and a pair of shorts which were a darker shade of the same colour. I had wanted some other shade but in XXL, the options were few. Getting ready for the gym is a little chore on all days. After all, if only the titles or the traits were sufficient, there wouldn't have been the ceremonial raiment and the paraphernalia. It's not just about getting into the gym wear and heading out. I have to carry my own towel and a bottle of water. The shoes too have to go inside the gym bag. Normally, they would be sitting under the tongue of the shoe and match my gaze by looking beyond the lining to confirm that they are there - my socks. But that day, I could see only gaping mouths with black throats. I lifted my shoes and tilted them to peek inside. Nothing. I then ran my palm on the inside of the shoes. "Where are the socks?" I exclaimed, silently.

If only one from the pair was missing, I would be looking hither and thither, under and over, left and right. Since both were missing,

Every Day is Another Day

the prudent thing to do was to look for a fresh pair of socks. My washed and clean socks are generally kept in one of the drawers in the closet in our bedroom. I switched on the torch light of my mobile phone. The wall closet is on the far side wall. The maneuver had to be delicate so as not to disturb the missus who was still sound asleep. I pushed open the sliding door on the right side of the closet. This side has shelves in the lower part. The top part is a wide and long section where my blazers and suits are hung. Right in the middle, dividing the upper and the lower parts, are two contiguous drawers. The one to the left is for things that need to be kept close at hand for those needs that arise occasionally like the small luggage lock and its key. The drawer to the right is for my socks – the long ones in Black, Blue and Grey that go with my formal office shoes, the long white cotton ones that I don't know why I have them, the ankle socks for the sneakers and the no-show socks for the slip-ons. I pulled open the drawer and directed the torch light inside. Instantly, I felt an intense fracture to my sense of gym fashion. Neither of the two pairs of ankle socks were there. A flicker ran through me carrying my own image in loose shorts reaching just above my knees and the white socks reaching them from below. The self-conjured image was too droll, even for me. I took out my Nike lower from the shelf below and discarded the shorts.

I put my shoes, water bottle, and towel in the gym bag, wore my FitBit, put one set of house keys in my pocket, slung the gym bag across my shoulder, wore my sandals, and came out of my flat. Standing alone in the corridor, I called for the lift and waited. In the silence of the morning, I could hear the drone of the lift when it moved. The lift arrived quickly. I entered it and pressed 'G' for the ground level. It was still a few minutes too early for the school going kids to start coming down with their respective mothers or fathers or both to wait for their school buses. The lift reached the ground floor quickly without stopping in between.

It was a few minutes minutes past six when I came out of the lift and walked out of my tower block. It had just about started to get bright. On the pavement, there already were some people doing their morning walks. Someone was jogging. I walked to the club house in a way that could be called insouciant.

As soon as I entered the gym, the chill hit me like unexpectantly. Mr.Deshpande is generally the first to arrive at six, and as soon as he enters the gym, he turns on the air conditioners. He is a heavyset man who perspires profusely and he would insist on all the four air conditioners being switched on and set at twenty-one degrees. Deshpande was on the elliptical cross trainer; as he would be every day. When I entered, he saw my reflection in the tinted glass partition separating the gym and the swimming pool. "Good morning", he shouted to my reflection raising his right hand. "Good morning", I replied. In a few minutes, the gym would be heaving with the rest of the morning regulars. If Arora and his wife come, the two will hop on the two treadmills and keep walking forever. In the last few days, I had outmaneuvered them completely by coming a few minutes earlier. The Aroras are a team. Even if one of the treadmills is taken, they would find either the elliptical trainers or the cycles to work out together as a pair.

After setting my gym bag in a corner, I pulled out my shoes, my water bottle and my towel. I put on my shoes and got on one of the treadmills in triumph. Made just for that, the panel of the treadmill has

Every Day is Another Day

a round depression in the left corner in which I put the water bottle. I put the towel in the long depression in the lower part of the panel, again, made just for that. I looked to my left and Deshpande looked to his right and our eyes meet. We just smiled at each other without the trouble of saying anything: Deshpande continuing to throw all his fours at the elliptical and I pressing the start button on my treadmill. In the gym, grumpiness is generally the mark and virtue of a regular.

I set the timer to twenty minutes and the speed at 5.5 Kilometers per hour, and started walking. Unlike the first time on the treadmill, I did not hold the side grips but left my hands free. I was just about four or five minutes into my walk when someone got on the other treadmill and started running straightway. I turned my head and saw someone who I had not seen before, not only in the gym but also otherwise. "Must be some new dweller, a tenant, or someone who has bought a flat recently", I thought. Finally, minding my own business, I looked straight and continued with my walk. I didn't notice Deshpande getting off the elliptical. In the meantime, the Aroras had come and they hopped onto the spin bikes. Some sounds that were a blend of clinks and grunts were coming from behind and the opposite end of the gym. That was Deshpande on 'leg press' and someone sliding plates for bench press. It wasn't going to be long from then before one of the iron pumpers would attach his mobile to the music system and start playing from his playlist peppy songs that enthuse by their beats alone with their words being largely dismissed. This has been profitably understood only by Punjabi singers whose songs find their place among English songs in gyms across India where only the dhik chik, dhik chik matters and not the dick who is singing.

The tread mill took about 15 seconds to gradually stop after the timer showed 00:00. The other guy was still running: Horse! I picked my towel and wiped my face. Picking my water bottle, I got off the treadmill. I moved a bit away and sat on the seat of the lats-pulley which was unattended then. I sipped some water and looked at the clock that is fixed above the door. It was very close to quarter to seven. I needed to get back home to be able to leave for office in an hour from then. I quickly removed my shoes, put them in my gym bag along with the water bottle and the towel, and come out. I took my sandals from the shoe stand and slipped into them. Coming down the small flight of stairs onto the pavement, I started walking towards my tower amidst the morning walkers, and a jogger or two. There were more people on the walkway compared to when I was coming to the gym. I reached the foyer of my tower. Mr.Swamy from the 16th floor was waiting for the lift with some flowers in a polythene bag in his hand; flowers that he had plucked from the plants on the driveway at the periphery of the complex.

"Hello Jee", he greeted me.

"Hello. Kaise hain Swamyji? (How are you Swamyji?)"

"Coming from morning walk?"

"No Sir, I am coming from the gym"

"Oh! I see. Exercise then?"

"No No. I just walk on the treadmill"

"Why? You don't like walking outside like us? Why go to the gym if one has to only walk?", he said with the air of a prig.

"It's not that. Just that in the gym, I get the feel", I said hiding my irritation.

Every Day is Another Day

"You are like South Indians in Chennai", he said like issuing a terse assessment witheringly.

"Why would you say so?", I asked him, once again hiding my irritation.

"You see, in Chennai, people eat Idli and Dosa at home and then, when they feel like eating out, they get ready, go to the famous Saravana Bhavan, and eat Idli and Dosa there. Now, why would they do so – go out and eat the same thing they eat every now and then at home?"

I just kept looking at Mr.Swami as I did not have an answer to his question.

"To get the feel", he said.

The lift arrived. I got in unamused, with Swamyji.

The Last Working Day

Monday is my rest day because on that day, the club house staff get its weekly off and it is kept shut for any maintenance work. On that day, without doing my morning walk, I went to my office.

It was like any other day at work. I was at my desk and so was Naveen in the cubicle across mine. It was somewhere around five in the afternoon that Naveen got a call on his cell phone. He picked it up on the second ring itself as though he was awaiting that call. "Just hold on for a minute", saying so, he walked out, and came back after some time that was longer than half an hour; that much, I was sure. While taking his seat, he looked at me and smiled.

"Where had you gone for so long?", I asked in a friendly way.

"Oh, nothing, wife had called", he said.

I wanted to but I did not ask "whose wife?". Now, on phone, who talks to one's own wife for so long? Clearly, he did not want to come straight and I did not insist. You know that I hate phonies too much to care even a bit about them except that I notice their shenanigans and this makes me hate them even more. In the course of the next few days, this happened a few more times. I could neither ask nor elicit much from Naveen. Between us, we were a little more than colleagues and a lot less than friends. People like us are called office buddies. Office buddies know each other's cars but don't know which houses the cars belong to. Office buddies drink together at the pub near their office on any day but on a Saturday or a Sunday.

Nearly ten days went by and then, out of the blue, Naveen resigned. Not that anybody briefed me on Naveen's quitting. Office grapevine was everyone's trusted broadcast; as the source as well as

Every Day is Another Day

the medium.

Now that things were quite in the open, I needed to speak with Naveen. I had to know a few things from him like where he was going, why he was going, and such. Not that I cared but these things make me curious. Since I carry my lunch that I prefer to eat at my desk, and I don't smoke which requires one to step out countless times with office buddies in tow, the chance to have a discreet conversation with Naveen was as difficult to find as it is impossible to find a half rich yet humble person. Also, I did not want to appear presumptuous. But then, there is always that coffee conversation over which, some leeway is well within good manners. I remember asking Naveen one day, at around four in the afternoon. He readily agreed. We took our coffees from the vending machine and went to the walkway on the first floor that ran around the office building. Not many were there in that late afternoon hour barring some smokers here and there standing close to some of the high metal ashtrays. We walked towards the corner and took our place to stand peacefully and have our coffee. The polite things had already been spoken while taking coffee and walking up to the elevator. I had to just resume the conversation and so, cutting the chase, I said with a bit of surprise , "Naveen Bhai, you have quit this job".

"Yes dear, how much more should I suffer here?", he replied in a more forthcoming manner than the smug nod or a simple yes that I was expecting. "And then bro, the dick talks so much shit that I can't take it anymore", he added

"Who?", I asked. I gagged and almost spilt my coffee when I heard Naveen say "Dikshit".

Sanjay Dikshit, our manager, is another phony who is a dork in the collective opinion of all of us who continue to wait for their much-deserved promotion while this phony gets set over us. Notwithstanding the sentiment, it was the appreciation for Naveen's ingenuity that rose suddenly from deep within that gagged me. I mean, describing Sanjay Dikshit, thus: the dick who talks shit. That was a class act. Anyway, Naveen continued. I was just not aware that in this mild inquiry of mine, I had opened the sluice gates.

"Look boss, I can't keep begging for a raise every year. And, what is this 'Met Expectations' that I get rated as in every appraisal cycle. Such an unimaginative and lowly assessment a man would not do even of the boyfriend of his daughter. And then boss, is this what you call a team with all the politics and the sucking that goes around? You tell me why should there be a review on Friday evening and then another one on Monday morning? This is sadism in the garb of management system. I am glad that I tried and I got another job quickly......blah blah blah."

I was gawking so much that my dentist could have sat inside my mouth. My coffee was over and I don't know how many times we went around the walkway that day with Naveen blithering and I just listening. After some while, I was earnestly hoping for Naveen to stop and I still don't remember when he did. Only one or two of the reasons he cited could have explained his leaving but he seemed to be telling me "pick as many as you like from the pile in front of you".

Finally, on a Monday, Dikshit called a brief team meeting to let us all officially know that Naveen had quit, the coming Friday would be his last working day with us, and there would be a farewell party in the evening.

On that Friday, I entered my office from the main foyer of the building to take the lift to the sixth floor. Unlike the other days when I would park in the basement and take the lift from there, that day, I had come by a taxi so that in the evening, after the drinks, I could return home in one without having to drive my own car in deference to the law of the land. Dikshit was paying for the party.

I was not upset about Naveen's leaving. If a colleague at the same level as yours leaves, you suddenly become the muscle to be retained than the fat you are that needs to be rid of. In job, security is not in numbers but, in the lack of it. And, in some way, I was looking forward to the party. I am not a phony to not accept that I like free meals and free booze. The irony though is that Dikshit was going to pay given what Naveen thought of him.

As I walked up to my cubicle, I noticed Naveen's laptop on his desk. I looked around but he was nowhere to be seen. After keeping my laptop bag on my desk, I pulled out my phone from my pocket to dial his number. On second thought, I decided otherwise. "He must've gone to the cafeteria for some tea or coffee", I thought. I settled in my chair and connected my laptop.

It must have been a couple of minutes only; while I was sifting through my mails, I heard some shuffling and I looked up. Naveen was entering his cubicle looking at an open diary in his hands. "Hey Naveen, don't set a bad example by working so hard on your last day here", I said when our eyes met.

Naveen entered his cubicle and walked up to his desk before leaning over the open partition to say "Boss, do you know what all one has to do before being relieved from the job? I was with the admin for the last thirty minutes and I am glad that I took my diary and pen with me because after the first few things she asked me to do, I knew that I won't remember all of them. I have noted not less than two pages of instructions. She is sending me an e-mail but I still noted it in the simple English that I understand. I think I am going to take at least three hours to complete all the formalities. After all that, I have to say goodbye as well to a lot of people."

"Phonies have this habit of making a mountain out of a molehill", I thought. "Okay Naveen, you go about your things. And, if you free up by lunch, call me. We will have lunch together", I offered and let Naveen go about his tasks.

It was around 1:15 PM. I was walking back to my cubicle from the meeting where a new project that had started recently was being reviewed. I was hungry. Naveen was not at his desk. I called him on his phone but he did not answer. I texted him on WhatsApp to ask about lunch because there was nothing phony about my offer. The message was delivered but the blue ticks didn't appear for some time. He was not seeing his messages. What more could I do? I opened my lunch box and started to eat.

Naveen came back to his desk at around 3 PM and took his seat. I did not notice him because I was in the middle of an office conference call where people from our different offices in Mumbai, Bangalore, and Delhi had joined. The call got over in a few minutes. I become aware of Naveen shortly when intermittently, people came and stopped by at his cubicle to have little chats. Someone leaving the job is always a matter of excitement for many in the company in a vicarious way like watching something erotic where someone else is having all the fun but it is the watchers who get excited. "Is there any end to this phony business?", I thought.

The rest of the day passed without any event. It was nearing 6 PM and I was glad that we were nearing end of the day, and I was looking forward to the party. Some people had already left for the day, it being a Friday. Just then, an e-mail arrived from Naveen carrying the subject 'My Last Working Day'. I opened the e-mail and read it.

Every Day is Another Day

While I have myself got many such e-mails yet, I never really imagined that one day, I will be writing one. Today is my last working day here. It is with a very heavy heart that I am bidding adieu to all of you. This place and the wonderful people around have left an indelible mark on me. The professionalism and the deep sense of values of this organization have brushed on me and they have changed me forever. I have learnt some of the best lessons of my professional life here among you. It will be with a great sense of pride that I will wear my experience here as a badge throughout the rest of my career.

It was a fun filled journey: these three years. I have made so many friends here who I would like to cherish for a long time. I thank you all wonderful and talented people from who I have learnt a lot and in seeing whose talents, I always felt humbled.

I would like to thank my manager Sanjay Dikshit for his constant mentorship and guidance. Sanjay, you are a wonderful person who I have always looked up to. I will be so glad to work with you again. Finally, I thank my team for their accepting me when I joined, their patience in letting me settle and learn and the deep sense of bonding that we developed that made each day in office a memorable one.

This is the best place one could ask for because it offers so much to do and learn, the leeway to commit mistakes without being judged and eventually, the confidence it builds in one.

I will terribly miss this place and all of you. So, thank you again for everything. Keep in touch.

Truly Yours,

Naveen Sharma

I read the e-mail again, and then one more time. Incredulous!

I was not soppy but I need to admit that Naveen's mail had affected me. Naveen couldn't have written this e-mail in passing. Every word, every sentence was looking weighed and then put. It was only then, that is, after reading and then again reading his email that I felt a tinge about Naveen's leaving.

I was unaware and still tipsy from his e-mail when Naveen came to my cubicle. He was holding his laptop bag. "Let us go and occupy the tables. It is Friday and we won't get any place if we don't go now. Sanjay and the rest of team will join shortly. I need to return the laptop as well", he said.

I got up while Naveen was also turning. I caught him by his shoulder. He turned his neck and gave it a vertical jerk that is the wordless way of asking "what happened?"

I pointed to my laptop to show him his e-mail that was open on the screen.

"You read it? How is it?", he asked as though it was some work of art.

"It's such a nice email Naveen. I did not know you could write so well. You really mean all the things you have written?", I asked.

"Of course, bhai, I am feeling so sentimental today. I had to express my feelings", he said.

"Naveen, until this e-mail, I did not know how much you loved our organization and all of us. You think so well about our team and especially about Sanjay. And, you are saying this is the best place. These feelings are fresh ones or, they were always there that got intensified today?", I asked.

"Bhai, what are you trying to say?", Naveen asked trying to be naïve which is the most common defence mechanism of phonies. Oh! how I hate phonies.

"If you really feel the way you have written, the point then is, why are you leaving?", I asked with a smile on my face to blunt the edge of the question.

I turned to shut my laptop and put it in my bag, winding up and readying for the party. I turned again to see Naveen still standing behind me. I saw that Naveen's dentist could sit inside his mouth. "Let's go and return your laptop first", I said.

Financial Wizard

After the farewell party, it was eleven thirty in the night when I reached home. For a moment, I thought of ringing the doorbell but decided against it, and opened the door with the key that I had: which I had taken with me knowing that I would be late. As soon as I entered, the missus sat up on the sofa. She was holding her iPad. "Come fast, Rashi is showing her house", the missus beckoned me to join her on the video call. Rashi is my sister-in-law who lives in Minnesota in the USA. As soon as I came in the frame, I could not see Rashi but saw a large bedroom with wooden flooring, a large bed (against a light Grey wall) with a very thick mattress on it, a large window with white frame, and through the glass, I could make out a large green lawn at the far end of which, there were tall trees through which, some water body, perhaps a small lake, was also visible. At that very moment, Rashi flipped the camera and came in the frame – staring at us up-close, holding her phone close to her face. "Jeejaji, kaise ho? I should not even talk to you. You never call us. You have never brought Didi and the children to USA. See, now we have bought a big family home also. When you all come, you will stay in the big room below. Wait, let me show you". She said all this in one breath and then flipped the camera back, keeping it focused down where I could see a light-coloured carpeted floor, and after some time, I could see some steps, which too were carpeted, Rashi was walking down them because in between, I could see a foot. The video call lasted another half an hour because Rashi started all over again to show us her new house. The missus was too involved in the house tour, especially the kitchen with its large size, the different gadgets in it, the refrigerator that was as big as our wardrobe, and going by her comments, I understood that she was seeing the kitchen all over again.

After the call got over, I got up and changed. When I came to bed, the missus was already in it, sitting at her corner, leaning on her left elbow that rested on two pillows. The moment I sat, the missus said "listen".

"Yes, tell me".

"How small our house is. Let us buy a bigger one with a big kitchen and large bed rooms."

"Haan, dekhte hain (alright, we will see)", I said, lied down, pulled the counterpane over me, and closed my eyes.

Taking the allowance that days of the weekend offer, the next day, I got up at around seven. The missus was already up. When I came out of the bedroom, I could see her in the living room. She was sitting on the sofa, holding her coffee mug in both her hands and staring straight ahead of her, immersed in some deep thought. As I walked inside the living room, the missus sensed my approach, blinked, looked at me, and as I was sitting down on the sofa, said, "Rashi's house is so good na." The missus is capable of starting a conversation in the morning exactly at the same point where she had left it last night before her going to bed as though she can just hit the pause button on the conversation and then hit play again on getting up. Hmm, I assented again. She made coffee for me, and brought it over, sat beside me, and asked "what do you think about Rashi's house?"

Before I could answer, she added "how big it is!". Hmm, I assented again after I took my first sip of coffee. The missus got flustered.

"What hmm, hmm you are doing? Can't you talk properly to

me?"

"Okay, yes, her house is very nice. All family homes in the US are like this"

"Can we also not buy a bigger house?"

"Dekhte hain"

But this time, 'dekhte hain' did not work. The missus was quick to retort "that is what you say for everything. Are you seriously going to look for a bigger place?"

"Arre yaar, we already have our home loan running on this house. Until I clear that, I am not discussing anything about any house", I said in a way that surprised me as well because I am never so curt with the missus because when she gets upset with me, she is capable of shutting me out completely which is a prospect I dread, but that day, for some strange reason, the missus remained normal and did not bring up Rashi's house or any other house.

I finished my coffee, and went inside to get ready for my morning walk.

I don't know why I got upset that day. The missus was simply asking me what any woman would do – ask her husband a nice and comfy home not because our house wasn't nice or comfy but because in certain things like a car, a house, the bank balance or, even the bed, the measure of their goodness is directly proportional to their size; the bigger, the better. I think I got upset because for people like me, a house always entails a loan, and this loan is a very nasty thing which I have been wanting to escape since the day I took it. While it gave me my house, as a recompense, it had been taking nearly a quarter of my salary every month, leaving me wanting in a lot of other things. Anyway, the matter of the new house was buried under our other

Every Day is Another Day

troubles until it popped up again like something does when the heavy object over it, that obscures it, is lifted.

After about a year, my fortunes changed because of two reasons. One was a chance investment in an insurance policy that I had made about eight years ago in which, I was made to pay a premium of fifty thousand rupees for the first three years only, which they invested in the stock market, and which matured after it ran its course, and this brought a few lakh rupees to my bank account. The second was because of the phony business of people. I was not happy with my dismal performance ratings and salary increments, I interviewed in a few places, got a job offer with a good increment, I resigned, and then, the phony people in my company let me know how valuable I was, they gave me a good hike and topped it with a decent retention bonus which, according to me was an amend to the wrong of the past, but the phony people took an undertaking from me that I will stay for at least another two years, and if I left before that, I will have to return the bonus amount. After I took two credits of the increased salary while the retention bonus sat in my account for a month already, on a Saturday, around noon, I parked my car a little away from the Chembur branch of HDFC Limited.

I took out my sling bag from the back seat, crossed it across my shoulder, locked my car and walked towards the branch with a little nervousness in anticipation of a large crowd there of loan seeking people. However, on entering the branch, I was surprised and relieved at the same time that there weren't many people in there. To my left, on the sofa, a small family: a man, his wife, and their very young girl, perhaps not more than five, was sitting. The lady was looking at a pamphlet while the man was minding their daughter. There were about five open cubicles in a straight line in front of me. The farthest two were unmanned. In the first one, a lady officer was behind the desk busy at her computer while the lady and the man sitting in front of her desk were busy signing some papers. In the next cubicle, a middle-aged man, accompanied by his teenaged son, was discussing something earnestly with the officer at the desk. In the third cubicle, the officer behind the desk was referring to some papers one moment and typing something in his computer in the next. Still surveying, as I turned my head towards my right, I saw the security guard. He was sitting in a metal chair looking at me without much expression. As soon as our eyes met, he asked "Kya kaam hai Sir". "I need to settle my loan", I told him. He asked me to fill a form before getting up and calling me to the small table to his right. He took the small booklet that was on the table and opened a page for me where I wrote my loan account number, my name, my phone number, and put my signature at the bottom. He tore the page and said "baithiye, bulayenge (please sit, you will be called)". I walked up to the waiting area and sat in the single sofa chair without bothering the man, his wife, and their little girl. There were some old editions of Indian Today and The Oultook magazines on the center table.

I was still intently reading when my name got called. I shut the magazine, kept it back exactly where it was earlier on the center table, and got up. "Third counter", the security guard, who was still in his chair, said to me. I walked along the narrow passage to the third cubicle. "Hello Sir, please sit", the officer said with a lot of amiability. "What can I do for you?", he asked the moment I sat in my chair and straightened after keeping my sling bag down, by the side of my chair. "I want to foreclose my loan account", I said. Still smiling, and now looking at the chit I had filled, he said "sure Sir". Referring to the chit, he punched some numbers in his computer which I reckon must have been my loan account number because a moment later, he said,

"I can see the account Sir". In the brief moment when the computer was busy in searching my account, I looked at the name plate on the table on which Swapnil Naik was written. Have you brought the loan agreement copy with you?", Swapnil asked me. I picked my sling bag and took out the thick file of the loan agreement copy and handed it across to him. After checking the file with his eyes darting one moment at the screen and the other at the file, Swapnil asked for my PAN Card which I gave to him. He beckoned the security guard and handed the card to him. "How much of the loan is still remaining?", I asked. "Sir, after you clear the current installment which is due in the next few days, your principal outstanding would be thirteen lakhs seven hundred", he said. By the time this inquiry was answered, the security guard came back with a photo copy and handed it over, along with my PAN Card, to Swapnil who first checked the photo copy, then returned my PAN card to me before picking up a pen from his desk that he pushed towards me along the table, together with the photo copy. "Please sign it Sir", he said. "Should I cut the cheque now?", I asked. "Just one second Sir, I will give you a statement and then you can write the cheque with the exact details", he said before once again doing something on his computer. The small printer on his desk came alive with some whirring and coughed out a paper which Swapnil pulled out from the tray, and handed it over to me. "Cheque should be in the name of?", I asked. "HDFC Limited. After that, write Loan Account, put a colon, and then write your loan account number. The cheque should be for the principal outstanding amount only. The last EMI, we will deduct from your bank account, as usual", he said. There were a few more formalities to be completed that were nothing but a signature here, a signature there, some checking on the computer, then checking it again; all done by the party that is receiving the money and appearing more cautious than when it was giving the loan perhaps because a loan is a sale whereas a foreclosure is a return of goods that no seller is ever prepared for as in expecting it to be a task for the day. Anyway, all this was now stretching my patience and amusing me at the same time.

As I was handing over the cheque to Swapnil on the other side of the desk, I was feeling an effusion of a relief, hitherto unknown to me. I was getting the feeling of being liberated. Swapnil scanned the cheque closely, just to make sure everything was alright. He printed a receipt, and after handing it over to me said "Sir, the original papers of your apartment will come here in ten to fifteen days. You can then come and collect them from here."

I nodded, and as I was getting up from my chair having already picked up my sling bag, Swapnil handed over his business card to me and said, "alright Sir, please let us know if there is anything else we can do for you?" "Thank you", is what I said bearing the smile of gratitude towards the invisible benefactor or the chance happenings that had put the bulk money in my bank account. I shook hands with Swapnil and started to walk back with a buoyant lightness: as a debt free man. I came out of the branch and breathed a new air which was in fact as stale as it always is with the pollution and odours Mumbai. I was feeling very happy because from the next month onwards, a large part of my salary wouldn't be going to service my mortgage, in my balance sheet, only tangible assets would appear and to balance it, my one hundred percent equity.

While I had put down the burden from my shoulders and I was walking straight and swelled yet, I was hungry. It was close to 1 PM, but not yet. After stepping out of the branch, I turned left, crossed Vagad's men's garments showroom, turned left again, and started walking towards Gita Bhavan. I stepped in and found the place to be not very crowded. I took a table for four that allows for keeping one's bag in the chair next to the one in which one sits, and if one orders well, allows for the plates, the cutlery, the salt and pepper, the tumbler of water and the tissue papers to be kept comfortably unlike the table for two which actually is suitable only for having coffee but to which people who come in pairs are forced to go when the bustle is high which was not the case when I entered Gita Bhavan. I scanned through the menu card and ordered for myself one 'Idli Vada Sambar' and a plate of 'Bisi Bele Bhaat'. The latter, I had picked a liking for from old my days in Bengaluru. The meal was quick. When the bill came, it's total, Rupees one hundred and sixty, I paid in cash and not by my credit card.

After the humble meal, I sat in my car to drive back home, which was a forty-five minutes' drive. As I started, I remembered Kamlesh, an investment advisor who had met me not a long while ago. Kamlesh had suggested that someone like me, on the right side of forty, with children aged around ten or twelve, should invest around twenty to thirty thousand every month in Mutual Funds for their futures, which were illuminated bright by Kamlesh's vivid descriptions about their education abroad and their grand weddings. It was a strange brightness to which my eyes didn't squint but opened wider. Kamlesh was so concerned about my children's future that had my children been around listening to him, they would've wanted him to be their father and not me. I couldn't heed Kamlesh's advice then but I still started a systematic investment plan for ten thousand. Now, I thought seriously about increasing my SIP by fifteen thousand. I had just about crossed Deonar, and I was moving towards Mankhurd. Fifteen minutes can be sufficient time when planning, undistractedly.

It was fifteen minutes past two when I parked my car in my

parking lot and went up to my apartment. The missus and the children had planned the 2 PM movie show at The Little World mall. They were to be back only by five in the evening. I stretched myself on the sofa and pulled my laptop. The new-found freedom and litheness were making me float and my feet rested on the center table. I leaned back. I opened my laptop and balanced it on my lap. I opened Hyundai's website, looking for a sedan. Accent would fit my requirement, and considering the buy back of my old Santro, in a few lacs more, it would come for which, I wouldn't have to take a car loan. The color would be dark grey. Before I could decide on the variant, I opened Thomas Cook's website and looked for some foreign vacations. I scanned for Singapore and Malaysia, Europe, Only Switzerland, Safari in Kenya. Considering the just about stopped cash outflow and the next four months after which the school vacations would start, I calculated that I could save enough for the Singapore and Malaysia option. I left my contact details on the Thomas Cook website and logged off. At this junction, despite the excitement, I felt like sleeping because that is also one of the many things one has to do and so, I put the laptop away and slept on the sofa. When I got up, it was already four. I made some tea for myself, stood by the balcony, and watching the sights outside through the window grill, drank my tea.

A little after five, when the doorbell rang and I opened the door, only the missus was there. After she entered the house, I asked about the children. She let me know that they met their friends as soon as they entered the community's gate, and went to play. Unlike me, the missus doesn't put her bag here or there. She walked inside the room, put her bag inside her part of the wardrobe, and came back to the living room. I was once again on the sofa. The missus walked towards the open kitchen and once there, asked me "chai piyoge?" I let her know that I had had my tea, to which the missus did not

Every Day is Another Day

say anything, made tea for herself, brought the cup with her, and sat beside me on the sofa. It was then that the conversation started.

"Finally, we are done with this home loan"

"So, all paid up?"

"Yeah. You know, what a relief it is?"

"I am sure"

"Accha, let us go out for dinner. I am very happy today"

"No, some other day. Today, I have already planned for methi paratha".

"Accha suno na, the bigger three-bedroom flat on the 7th floor is up for sale. Mrs.Gupta told me. The owner is some Girish. This was an investment flat of his. I heard he is asking ninety lacs. Why don't we buy it?"

"Arre, why do we need another house? For us, this is sufficient. We already have three bedrooms."

"Which three bedrooms do we have? Ours is 'two and a half'. What you call the third bedroom is actually a just a small study room."

"For the four of us, this is good enough",

"But parking is for one car only na! Once you get me my Alto, whenever that is, where will we park?"

"We will figure that out. And, does one buy a flat to get parking? Kuch Bhi bolti ho yaar!"

"That is not the point. Children are growing. They need their own rooms and this house is too small."

"You know in Mumbai, a family larger than ours stays in a one-bedroom flat"

"Don't talk non-sense"

"And, during the school vacations, Rashi and her children will come to stay with us for two weeks. Where will they stay?"

"They are family yaar. We will adjust in the bedrooms and the drawing room"

She just gave me a straight look for a few moments and without saying anything, turned, and walked inside. "Where have you gone? Say something", I said just loud enough so that she could hear me but without the appearance of shouting. "So, every time guests come, we need to adjust? That is what you are saying. After all, what have I done all these years other than adjusting with you", she said coming out again to the drawing room but stopping at the dining table to adjust the trivets on it, appearing to be speaking to herself than to me.

"But guests come once in a while. What about the other days? It will be waste only no!", I tried to reason.

"Why do you wear your helmet every time you take out your bike?", she asked me but this time looking at me.

"What has that got to do with this?", I asked with some irritation.

"It has. If you don't want to answer, leave it", she said.

"I wear the helmet so that if I fall, I have the chance to remain safe", I replied.

"Do you fall every time you ride?", she asked next.

"Who falls every time he rides a bike?", I answered, again with a straight face thinking about the futility of this line of conversation.

"The helmet will save you on that one day you might fall. So, according to you, it is a waste of money on all the other days", she said.

In my stupefaction, I remained silent for a few seconds. My defense seemed to have been breached. In my nervousness, I made a fatal mistake. I said "But it will not happen that fast. First, we will have to find a buyer for this house."

While the vanquished has to lick his wounds immediately, the victor can take his time to savour the victory. "Accha, you sit. I will quickly make some bhajia", she said leaving me and the conversation at that point from where both couldn't move until she returned.

I was on the sofa all this while, and I started fiddling with my phone. Soon enough, she returned with bhajia in a steel plate. She handed over the plate to me before sitting next to me. "Suno na, why do we have to sell this house? We have two children. Don't we need at least two houses? We can stay in one and rent out the other. We get to invest and we get regular income also", she said.

The vehemence had already gone out of me. Meekly, I said "just now we could manage to clear this loan. Before that, there was the loan on the Pune flat. What I am thinking is that we should start investing in mutual funds from the money we would be able to save from now on. They appreciate steadily over the years and we can easily liquidate them, in part or in full. Then, let us enjoy with the extra money."

"See, that is the problem. If it is easy to liquidate, you will use them before they appreciate enough. Price of the flat will also appreciate na. That Girish would have bought this flat for not more than fifty lacs and see, in five years, he is getting ninety. The rent that we will get, we can invest that", she said parrying my rationale.

"That is true. But, fifty becoming ninety is fine. How will ninety again appreciate at the same rate?", I tried to counter.

"Everything happens", she said dismissively.

"But from where will we get ninety lacs and then another at least ten to spend on the woodwork, paint work etc., that we will have to anyway do?", I asked her.

"They are there no", she said.

"Who?", I asked earnestly.

"HDFC, ICICI, SBI"

"Alright Sir, please let us know if there is anything else we can do for you?", Swapnil had said.

I did not know on that morning that I will have the need to call him back so soon. His business card was still in my wallet. The home loan seemed to have no plan to ever leave me.

Listening to Ghazals

I wasn't too keen about the 7th floor apartment, and so, I never brought it up on my own in any conversation with the missus. She however, kept reminding me whenever she would remember about it in between the usual busyness of life. On one Sunday, at about four in the afternoon, when the missus was coming up in the elevator, joining her from the ground floor, a middle aged couple and another man also got in, this other man was holding a thick bunch of keys from which he pulled out a smaller set of three keys, which the missus noticed, and as she is quite capable of making a small conversation with anyone, she probed a little bit, and got to know that the couple had come to see the 7th floor apartment, and the other man with the keys was the property agent.

I was in the bedroom watching TV when the missus rang the doorbell. When I opened the door, she entered the house seeming quite restless. She dumped the bag she was carrying on the dining table, turned towards me, and said "you have still not called Mr.Girish. Now property agents have also started bringing people to see that house. Are you ever going to call him? Nobody listens to me in this house. I had given you his number after taking it from Mrs.Gupta. I had to tell her we are interested in that house. She still keeps asking me about it. How embarrassing it is for me. But who cares…..". The missus, while she was still breathing hard, looked up for an old SMS from Mrs.Gupta, retrieved Girish's number from it, and asked me to talk to him then and there.

In a much-accelerated way, we bought this larger apartment within two months of my calling Girish on the aforesaid day. Girish was happy to sell to us bypassing the broker, he did not have to give us any concession because I am bad at negotiating, HDFC was very happy to extend a new loan to me as I was one of its good customers who had foreclosed two loans in the past, and notwithstanding my reservations about another home loan, we too were happy because normally, any new thing brings happiness. By the way, we did not shift to the bigger house because the missus said "in a few months, children will have their exams, I don't want to disturb their studies". Then, the exams got over, a few days after which, my sister-in-law and her children visited us, she came from Pune where she went first after coming from the USA, and we adjusted in our old apartment very well with my sleeping in the living room: on the couch, all the four children in their room, and the missus and her sister sleeping in ours.

After about a week, on the next weekend, it was time for the sister-in-law to return to Pune. On that Sunday morning, we hired a taxi and took my Santro as well because we were seven people in all. The missus, my sister-in-law, and her elder boy sat in the taxi while both my children and my sister-in-law's younger boy joined me in my Santro. We drove down to Pune starting at around six thirty in the morning, reaching my in-law's house by around nine. While the plan was for the missus and the children to stay back in Pune for a week, I was to return to Mumbai the same evening because I had to attend office the next day.

When we reached Pune, an elaborate breakfast was already ready on the dining table which is always there for sons-in-law which I think is a well thought out social custom to keep them well reminded that they are guests not by the directness of words which may be seen as an affront but by such a subtle indication that could be managed with a sumptuous repast because it is only when guests are expected that the fire in the hearth burns the longest. The missus and her sister walked

146   *Every Day is Another Day*

straight in to keep their bags inside. The attention of the grandparents was directed mostly towards the children and I took to the sofa to watch TV. I wasn't paying much attention to the happenings around me and sat by myself which is an acquired skill in image management because while there are many worthy compliments to earn like "he is a lot of fun to be around", "oh! he talks so well", "oh! he is so nice", there is none that compares to this where your in-laws are forced to say "he doesn't speak much. Such a simple boy!"

By the time the breakfast was done, that is to say that even the missus, my sister-in-law, and my mother in-law had eaten after feeding the children, during which time, I and my father-in-law were in the drawing room having a conversation which was mostly inquiries from him to which I was answering, it was close to fifteen minutes past ten. I looked at my watch. "It would be good for me if I left now", I thought before I stood up and told my father-in-law that I would be leaving. Even before my father-in-law could complete his perfunctory protest, my mother-in-law, who, perhaps had overheard this conversation, rushed out of the kitchen and said "no, you can't leave now. Lunch is being made. You can't leave without having lunch" in a decisive way which was buttressed by the missus who was standing behind her, who did not say anything but just outstared me when I looked at her for some support. When outnumbered thus and still playing up to my image of a simple boy who doesn't speak much, I sat back. Just then, my father in-law got up and said "I will go, you take some rest", which was his way of saying that it was in fact time for him to take rest and since he couldn't ask me to leave him alone, decided to leave me alone to go to his room. Whichever way it came, I was best when left to myself. After my father-in-law left, I fiddled with the remote until I found a channel on which I could watch something on the TV. Somewhere in between, that is before lunch, I called Venky. "Venky, the evening plan is still on, right?", I asked. "Yes, yes, I will reach by seven", he said. "You want me to bring anything?", he asked. "No, everything will be ready, you just come. I will be waiting", I said before hanging up.

It was 2 PM by the time the lunch was done and I was ready to leave, this time without any protestations other than the disappointment expressed by everyone but the missus on my not staying over but which was managed by me by not giving a dubious excuse like a rookie (like I did not want to drive back after it is dark, or that later on a Sunday evening, traffic would be much on the highway) but by giving a very credible reason that the pest control folks were coming at 5 PM for which someone had to be at home, to which the missus said "but you did not tell me", to which I said "oh!, I forgot, they had called yesterday to fix the appointment." After I reached Mumbai, I did not turn right on the highway to enter Kharghar but continued straight to Belapur where there are liquor stores. At Belapur, I bought eight bottles of beer. On my way back home, close to our apartment complex, at a general store, I bought some savouries to bite with the beer. Finally, I parked my car inside our compound and reached home with the bags of goodies for the evening. It was thirty minutes past five. I went straight to the kitchen and stacked the beers inside the refrigerator.

There was a good amount of time to kill before Venky came. I made some tea for myself and stood in my balcony to have it. After the tea, there was still more time to kill. Therefore, I waited out by watching on YouTube some famous innings of Sachin Tendulkar. It is amazing how quickly time passes when one is watching even bits of old games of cricket. It was six thirty now. I pinged Venky on WhatsApp. "Leaving in ten, will be there by seven", he replied. I had just enough time now to shower and get ready. It took me fifteen minutes to quickly shower and get in my shorts and t-shirt. Very soon, it was seven, and I was already very eager for Venky to come. My doorbell rang just inside ten minutes after seven, and when I opened the door, there, standing with a broad smile and holding a polythene bag in his right hand, stood Venky. "What is that?", I asked like an old friend who cuts all the niceties and pleasantries and comes straight to the point. "Anda Bhurjee", he replied as he walked in. "Arre, but why? I have already got a lot of snacks", I said from behind him after closing the door. "Bhurjee tastes good with beer", he said while taking off his shoes in the vestibule between the main door and my living room, walked further inside the living room (I was walking behind him), kept the polythene bag on the centre table, and made himself comfy on the sofa before asking "you have got chips na?" "Yes, chips, moong daal, roasted cashews, namkeen mixture, all are there", I said before adding "should we start?" "Yes buddy", Venky said before both of us got up. Venky picked up the bhurjee and walked beside me to the kitchen.

Venky plated the bhurjee in a steel plate that he took out from the kitchen drawer. "Where are the spoons?", he asked. "See there, on the dining table", I said. By this time, I had taken out two bottles of beer from the refrigerator, picked up the bottle opener that I had already kept on top of it, opened the bottles, and walked back to the sofa where Venky was already plonked after keeping the plate of bhurjee on the centre table. I passed one bottle to Venky and then sat in the chair that was at right angle to the sofa. This way, we could see each other and talk while Venky could have the sofa to himself. The glasses or beer mugs were irrelevant in our setting where, the best way to enjoy the beer is to hold the bottle by its stout body, cover its narrow mouth with yours, push the head back while lifting the bottle to take large swigs first before they become sips after the first bottle is emptied by which time, the comestibles and the beer have become a bloating mixture in the stomach when the effervescence of the beer and the spices of the snacks dance together. We clinked our bottles by way of doing but not actually saying 'cheers', and took the first swigs. I sat back in the chair holding the bottle now by its neck and resting its bottom on the armrest of my chair while Venky kept his bottle on the centre table, took a spoonful of bhurjee, put in in his mouth, and before he could chew and swallow the thing said, "get the mixture and the chips". "Just a minute", I said before I kept my bottle as well on the centre table. From the kitchen I brought packets of Balaji Potato Chips and Haldiram Mixture, and placed the packets on the centre table. Venky rubbed his hands together and tore open the packet of chips. He pulled out one, put it in his mouth, munched it, which is when it made that exact crunchy sound when the thin slice of fried potato, that has grains of salt sticking to it, is bitten, and exactly then, the auditory sense adds to the confluence of the olfactory sense and the sense of the palate to make the potato chips the king of all snacks. While still munching, Venky passed on the packet to me. Once settled this way with the beers and the snacks, we started to talk of things that can be safely classified as trivial but which, with streaks of reminiscence, nostalgia, some plan for the future, with some sudden digression to the topics of politics or the economy, have their meaning in the present which is the joy of talking to a friend without any care for the world. In this way, the first bottle got over. When the second came, so came the roasted cashew nuts with it that are picked one at a time and savoured slowly unlike the chips that are stuffed in the mouth, or the mixture that is taken by the fistfuls, or the bhurjee that is taken by the spoonfuls, and they came just at the right time when the drinking was at an even keel.

"Put on some music man", Venky said. "What would you like to hear?", I asked. "Put some Ghazals", he said. I said "Okay", opened my laptop which is always close at hand, picked up my JBL Bluetooth speaker from the shelf next to the TV, and connected it to the laptop. I opened Youtube. From among the list that that had popped up on YouTube, I clicked on that famous one and anon, Jagajit Singh started to croon 'Huzoor aapka bhi ehtaraam karta chaloon, idhar se guzra tha socha salaam karta chaloon....'. Venky, who was making this 'wife away' day a 'Mehfil', started to sway to the music with closed eyes. My own bliss from this soulful music was blighted by the interference from the visuals of Venky's enjoyment that I was getting to witness because Venky is a South Indian who grew down South before the compulsion of career brought him here, where I was, and being so, had only a passable understanding of Hindi by which account, one could safely say that his understanding of Urdu was zilch. I couldn't stop myself from asking "Hey Venky, do you even understand what he is saying?". "Why do you ask man?", Venky asked me back. "Hey, are you getting the lyrics?", I questioned him again with the persistence we sometimes show even in a wrong line of questioning. Venky said 'it's so nice buddy – the music'. "What about the music? Don't you need to understand what is being sung?" I asked. "Why? The music is so nice, not at all loud but mild, just a few instruments, and such a sweet voice. I get that he is flirting with someone. Why do I even need to know exactly what is he saying?", answered Venky. I did not say anything further because, the finality of the answer awed me into that kind of silence that a denouement entails which, in a streak of genius and yet remaining unaware of it, Venky unraveled which was that it was the music and the way the Ghazal was rendered that were important, if you understood the words, you enjoyed the cherry as well, otherwise, the pastry was nice anyway.

Like a contrail, the episode stayed with me, and one day, the slight Urdu I possess, for the poetic language that it is, like that emotion that first rises from the pit of the stomach, then grips at the throat before bursting out like a sob, I said

"Zindagi ki mashabiyat Ghazal se hai,

Maynon me nahi, to tarunnam se maza leejiye."

(Life is like a Ghazal; if you don't understand the meaning, take pleasure from the melody.)

Let us talk again:

I am strolling in a mall - alone. I have come here to pick a book from Crosswords which is a very acceptable reason to be allowed to come to a mall all by myself. Before stepping out of the house, I had simply said "I am going out to pick some books from Crosswords". "When will you be back?", is all the missus wanted to know. I just wanted to pick a book; nothing in particular. The book shop is on the second level of the mall where the ground level is marked zero. There are a lot of people waiting for the elevator. I pass them giving them a passing thought reprovingly, and decide to take the escalator to reach the second level. It is like being frustrated in traffic in the exacerbation of which, I too am a part but only the others seem responsible for the hold up. I realize I am doleful today. Maybe, I have read some good books in the past few days. Good books have dollops of sorrow. I will need a cup of strong coffee afterwards, I decide. I am in an orbit distant from my normal station. Simply put, I am feeling blue, in general. I have a steady job, a steady family, some money in the bank, a house to live in and two that are leased out, a decent car. That means the mundane has been well taken care of, and finding the time and the resources, of its own accord, my mind is drifting towards existential problems. The problems that I am talking about are of the kind which, if you discuss with someone, you will get a shrug, a surprised look and the question 'what exactly is your problem?'. The mall is called In-Orbit.

I pick a couple of books that are contemporary now but future classics. They come from the Booker shortlist of this year and the last. I come out of the book shop holding my books in my right hand, the fingers bearing them and the cup of the palm supporting them;

the way I used to hold my records in school. I had declined the paper bag for which they were charging extra. I come down to level zero using the escalator that is running adjacent to the one that I had taken to get to the book shop. Starbucks is right in front of me, and I enter it. I order my black coffee: Sumatra, pour-over, before taking a small table for two in one of the corners. I plan to read about ten to fifteen pages with my coffee. The best way to finish anything is to start it as soon as you can. I unlock my phone. There is the new message notification of WhatsApp. Reflexively, I open WhatsApp. Someone or the other has a constant need to communicate with me and I cannot be cold to this reaching out. Aristotle just said so but WhatsApp made me understand that I am a social animal. I am part of more groups than the individual people I know. There are three messages in the group of school friends. I don't risk opening these in a public place. The paternal side of the family is discussing an upcoming wedding in the family and the maternal side is reacting to holiday pictures that one of the cousins has posted. While I am still scrolling, my name gets called. I go to the self-serve counter where the barista is all too nice having put my coffee on a tray and saying 'enjoy' while pushing it towards me. I bring over the tray to my table and let the coffee settle for a few seconds. I look around to see quite a few people, some chatting, some working on laptops, some talking on phones and some, just enjoying their drinks, coffee or otherwise. All the while, there are people entering and leaving. I look out of the glass walls and there are people around in the mall strolling, taking selfies, moving in and out of shops. I get a thought. It would, in a few moments turn out to be an awakening but not of the kind where one exults at the denouement but one where the misery becomes more acute, all options close, and the back is to the wall; the feeling of helplessness. Here I am, with the consciousness of my existence and here there are all these people, who are taking no notice of me. I feel my body going up and high very fast and very far having a distant yet clearly perceptible view of the things and the people around me. I am not just seeing. I am feeling like a witness to a constant happening. I am just one of the many with an incidental existence, it appears, not just among the many people who are here now but also among people in the preceding and the ensuing times. I don't have a grip on any of this all-around happening. My existence does not matter and so will my vanishing have no effect at all. I can't even call myself a small part of a big machine for, even a small part going bad can stop a big machine. A picture on the wall may go unnoticed by the people passing by it until the day it is removed leaving a bright patch on the very wall calling everybody's attention. I am not even such a picture; having the ability to become conspicuous by my absence. Depressing. Mind you reader, I have already told you that I am doleful today. I zoom in back and fiddle with my phone to access the collective knowledge on Google. I find that we are nearly seven and a half billion living right now, and over a hundred billion have already lived before us. That is a massive turnover of souls. When I know of the scale, things become even more melancholy for me. I wonder of my worth in this continuous sea of existence. I cannot get myself up to start reading. I am grappling with an existential crisis.

My mind is racing in many directions. Entropy is perched high here. But I am conscious of this whirlwind in my mind, and I am sure that some stable order will emerge eventually.

Is there something called self-assessment? That is what I am doing. In a quaint way, it can be called soul searching. Search is always of something that is lost; that which could not be found. So, is the self, lost, and it could not be found? This is the confusion.

Confusion doesn't sound right. Expression has to be forged on the anvil of words to make the simple mellifluous. No, the right word is conundrum. How can I be lost to myself? I am not lost. When I search for myself, I find someone small and lacking instead of someone more substantive I was hoping for. Like most of the things, this is relative - the feeling. It is a feeling because that is what it is. The self is inside me and therefore, it is not tactile.

I have read and heard about great people: men and women. Conquerors, philosophers, writers, scientists, strategists, leaders, businesspersons, sportspersons. Achievers. This knowing is also knowledge. You can sometimes be in awe of the things you know: not only the number of things but also the magnitude of each thing. In the mélange, people are also things. A great mountain does not make me feel small. A great person does. Comparison is among likes only. What do they say – "apples to apples". I don't matter because I am mediocre.

I recall my days in school when my parents would come to the parents-teachers conferences where I too would be present: standing behind my parents with my head bowed down but feeling the gaze of my teacher, every now and then. Always, the reference would be to my potential that I wouldn't use, and how intelligent I was and that I needed to only work harder to get better grades. These days though, I seem to be agreeing with my teachers. I think I have stayed in that liminal space always. For my family, relatives, friends, and acquaintances, I have done well for myself. That means I stayed on the expected course. For me though, I am just part of a crowd. Even in this mediocrity, there are people who are far ahead of me because they worked harder. The ones who worked harder and also used their potential are out of the common on their different course. I am frustrated. I don't really know what it is, how it is but, if it is, it has to be something like this - the midlife crisis.

I don't read the book. My plan has gone awry because of the musing. I finish the coffee but that hasn't helped me feel better. I pick my glum self and walk out of Starbucks. Walking the long length of the mall towards one end, I reach where the departmental store is at the basement level. That makes it easier for the shoppers to push their laden trolleys to their cars. There is a small escalator here that I take to descend which puts me right in front of the store. I turn left and walk out into the parking lot. I walk towards the pillars marked F to find the pillar F58 close to which, I had parked. I had noted the pillar number earlier. One learns such tricks to keep one's orientation in vast spaces like this parking lot. There are always an awful lot of cars here, parked in rows after rows.

I drive back home in about twenty minutes. I park my car in my designated parking slot in our apartment complex. I pick my books from the rear seat and walk inside the entryway towards the elevators where there is no one on this Saturday late afternoon. The languid security person is busy watching some video on his mobile phone. I worry for our security. The elevator door opens.

The missus opens the door and looks at my feet to make sure I have removed my sandals. I have. She lets me in. "Will you have tea? I was about to make some.", she says. I nod.

I put the books on the center table and go to the balcony outside our living room. It faces the quadrangle enclosed by the many buildings in our complex. The quadrangle has a lawn with children's play area and the club house with the gymnasium, swimming pool, a recreational area and the games room. The outer side is a wide paved track where people stroll, walk, jog or simply sit in the evenings on the stone benches at the lawn's edges. In the vesper light, the view is serene. Some children are cycling. In fact, they are racing. One boy is ahead: leading, with the others cycling hard to catch up with him. From the height that I am watching them, it is exciting to watch. They are going in laps. Momentarily, I lose who is leading and who is chasing because they are going in circles. But the boy who appears to be leading is leading for sure. He is leading because there are others behind him. Or, are the others behind him because he is leading? This is relativity. Physics and philosophy are mixing in my mind. The ecstasy of the winner has to stand on the misery of the losers. Without losers, there is no winner. Such thoughts are crossing my mind. "Here, take your tea. It's fun to watch from here, the children play", the missus says, pulling me out of my reverie. "What are you thinking?", she asks. "Nothing", I say. She has found fun where I am grabbing some drab. Who found the treasure? I think you can tell.

My kind reader, if you paying keen attention, you would have realized that I just had not one, not two, but three epiphanies separated only by a few moments. The first one is that I am a nobody, and the second one is that 'nobody' counts a great deal in the making of 'somebody'. Mediocrity is the bedrock of excellence. Excellence stands on mediocrity after first emerging from its midst. What is a leader who does not have scores who cannot themselves lead? What is a conqueror if there are not the scores who get vanquished? Usain Bolt who ran the race alone. Can that ever be?

While having tea, standing in our balcony, we are talking about things, about this and that, about here and there. I am feeling pleasant after watching the children. Unlike when I was in the mall and some trail of thought put me as just someone in the crowd; about which I became sad, I am now at ease with my mediocrity. The general may get feted for the victory, but I am thinking of myself as one of the unsung soldiers who fought. You may win the race but I too would have run without which, you the winner, will not find your glory. No, I am not saying that I give up. It is just that I have realised the important role I play in the discovery of excellence. This is also not to say that I won't keep trying. But I too will need losers if and when I win. So, I have a new found respect for them and concomitantly, for myself.

Like the cycle racing children, the happenings around me can be teachers. Every day is likely to have profound experiences and lessons for me, if only I pay attention. This is what I am going to do and collect vignettes that some good days will show me. Some, I have shared with you. For them to be appealing and to not give you cognitive stress, I have presented these with the ways of a raconteur.

"Hey stop, where is the third epiphany?", you are eager to ask here. I know. Remember, she found fun. That is the third one. What you get is what is you see.

I remember Charlie Chaplin here who said "Life is a tragedy when seen in close-up, but a comedy in long-shot". Comedy, because from a long shot, you see disparate happenings, connected and disjoint at the same time, meaningless yet so meaningful. From close-up, there is no perspective, one is too engrossed, like the blind men who got busy with the different parts and got very serious in going about them, who could never make out that it was an Elephant, and so, they were never amused by what they had actually found. Sum of parts is different than the whole. However, dear Madam/Sir, I am going to take life in pieces to have neither one close-up nor one long-shot. I want to amuse myself (and you) in myriad ways. For me, every day will be another day with its own sights, sounds, smells, lessons, and most of all, its own amusements.

Printed in the USA
CPSIA information can be obtained
at www.ICGtesting.com
LVHW040142150224
771722LV00003B/72